MICHAEL FARADAY

MICHAEL FARADAY

Father of Electronics

Charles Ludwig

HERALD PRESS
Scottdale, Pennsylvania
Waterloo, Ontario

Library of Congress Cataloging-in-Publication Data

Ludwig, Charles, 1918-
  Michael Faraday, father of electronics.
  Bibliography: p.
  1. Faraday, Michael, 1791-1869. 2. Physicists
—Great Britain—Biography. 3. Science—History.
I. Title: Father of electronics.
QC16.F2L82   530'.092'4 [B]   78-15028
ISBN 0-8361-3479-6

The paper used in this publication is recycled and meets
the minimum requirements of American National Standard
for Information Sciences—Permanence of Paper for
Printed Library Materials, ANSI Z39.48-1984.

MICHAEL FARADAY, FATHER OF ELECTRONICS
Copyright © 1978 by Herald Press, Scottdale, Pa. 15683
    Published simultaneously in Canada by Herald Press,
    Waterloo, Ont. N2L 6H7. All rights reserved
Library of Congress Catalog Card Number: 78-15028
International Standard Book Number: 0-8361-3479-6
Printed in the United States of America
Cover illustration by James Ponter
Design by Alice B. Shetler
07 06 05 04 03 02 01 23 22 21 20 19 18
Over 35,000 copies in print

To order or request information, please call
1-800-759-4447 (individuals); 1-800-245-7894 (trade).
Website: www.mph.org

for
Werner Kramer
who helped when help
was needed

CONTENTS

AUTHOR'S PREFACE

Less than two hundred years ago, the possibilities of electricity were as little known to mankind as cube root is to a gorilla. Even distinguished scientists knew practically nothing about this "slave" that now lights cities, browns toast, and flings images onto television screens.

In the midst of this ignorance, a wretchedly poor family moved to a London slum in 1791. (This was a year before Kentucky was admitted to the Union). As James and Margaret Faraday unloaded their shabby furniture and carried it into rooms in Surrey, few onlookers paid any attention. The reason was obvious. James Watt had perfected the steam engine; and since this "devilish monster" had put many out of work, the unemployed were migrating like ants into the city on the Thames.

To the nearly one million Londoners, the Faradays were just another family of nearly starved unfortunates. Nevertheless, that same year on a muggy September 22, Michael was born to them. And because of him our electronic age slowly squirmed into being. Indeed, his birth was one of the significant events of that century.

The London of this period was a sprawling city overflowing with filth, disease, and ignorance. Gutters were laid in the centers of the streets, water mains were built of wood, the streets were either dark or lit with candles or oil lamps, the police wore stovepipe hats, and sewage was channeled into water that was later used for drinking.

Since Louis Pasteur was not born until 1822, no one understood the danger of germs. Indeed, typhoid was not identified until 1880. Doctors—and barbers—operated without anesthetics and without sterilizing their instruments. Most surgical patients died.

According to statistics, Michael's chance of reaching ten was 27.7 percent; and his parents' chance of attaining seventy—figuring from the time of their births—was a mere 5.9 percent.

Schooling was reserved for the rich. Since Michael's mother could neither read nor write, education was not emphasized in their home. After he became famous, Michael remembered: "My education was of the most ordinary description, consisting of little more than the rudiments of reading, writing, and arithmetic. . . . My hours . . . were spent at home and in the streets." He had a passion for marbles!

The Faradays were members of the Sandemanian denomination. This devout group of Christians had broken away from the Church of Scotland. Since in the England of the time, those who did not belong to the Church of England were considered dissenters, the Faradays were scowled at by many of their neighbors.

In addition to his poverty and unpopular faith, Michael Faraday was seriously handicapped with an annoying speech impediment. He could not pronounce the letter *r*. The odds against him succeeding at anything in life were formidable. And yet, in spite of all this, he discovered the secrets which made both the electric motor and the electric generator possible. Many consider him the world's greatest experimental scientist. So far, more biographies have been written about this son of an ailing blacksmith than about Isaac Newton and Albert Einstein!

Albert Einstein was a devoted admirer of Faraday. While still in Berlin, this famous man who developed the theory of relativity kept a large portrait of Faraday in his study. Later, having escaped the Nazis, Einstein again displayed a large portrait of Faraday—this time in his Princeton study. Einstein believed that Faraday stood shoulder to shoulder with Galileo and Sir Isaac Newton.

Michael lacked formal education. He never learned—or at least he didn't remember—that all sentences should begin with a capital letter. This is so even though he had a very orderly mind and wrote thousands of letters. But he made up for this lack with an iron discipline and the unwavering faith taught to him by his parents and the devout elders of his church.

Charles Ludwig
Tucson, Arizona

Michael Faraday

Father of Electronics

1

DROPOUT

Snake eyes flashing, the lady schoolteacher slowly uncoiled, stepped from behind her rickety desk—and strode forward.

The children watched these signs of a forthcoming explosion with hidden amusement—and caution. From long experience they knew their teacher was about to strike. But since there was no reliable way to predict the victim, each was as wary as a cornered mouse without a hole.

For three painful seconds the tiny, cobwebbed room was silent as death. Finally, while twenty sets of eyes were glued to her hawklike features, the teacher exploded: "Michael Faraday, step forward!"

Although Michael had halfway expected to be the day's victim, the anger in her voice so frightened him, he scrunched even lower into his three-legged, unpainted chair.

"Michael Faraday!" she repeated even louder. "Have you no ears? Step forward at once!"

Forcing himself to obey, Michael stood quivering in front of her like a mouse in the claws of a cat. "Y-yes ma'am?" he managed, his gray eyes on the unswept floor.

"What's yer name?" she snarled.

From a corner of his eye, Michael noticed that her eyebrows had started to merge. This meant danger. It made him hesitate.

"Well, what is it?" she insisted.

"Fawaday." Michael tried so hard to pronounce the *r* his eyes squeezed shut.

"Fawaday! Fawaday! Fawaday!" she mocked, her thin lips whitening with rage.

Michael tried unsuccessfully to wink back the tears. It seemed everyone was against him! The richer children ridiculed his patches; others scorned his religion; and still others scoffed at his odd-shaped head.

"And what's yer brother's name?" she sneered.

"His name is W-W-Wabet Fawaday."

"And yer mother's maiden name?"

"Mawgwet Hastwell."

"And your baby sister's name?"

"Mawgwet—Meg to us."

"Why don't you ask him his oldest sister's name?" shouted the school bully from the back.

"Elizabeth," replied Michael, even before she asked.

The teacher glared in silence. Then, cupping her square chin in the V of her hand, she said, "I really don't know what to do with you. I've made you stand in the corner. I've made you wear a dunce cap. I've had you rocked in the cradle. I've made you kneel on bits of stone. I've slapped yer face and pulled yer ears. I've—"

"Give him a floggin'!" sang out the bully.

"Yes, I think I'll give you a floggin'," she announced grimly.

"Oh, please don't do that," begged Michael, remembering that he was wearing no underclothing to soften the blows. "It ain't that I don't want to speak wight—" Tears interrupted his speech. "It's just that I can't. Please. . . ."

"You can if you want to," she humphed. "anyway a good floggin' won't do you no harm." She noisily rummaged through the drawers of the desk for a cane. Unable to find one, she untied a handkerchief and withdrew a halfpenny. "Here, Robert, take this to the store and buy me a stiff cane. Michael's a-gonna say *r* even if I have to scorch his hide, rub it with salt, and hang it on the fence!"

Instead of going to the store, Robert ran home and reported to his mother.

Half an hour later the door burst wide, and Mrs. Faraday with Robert at her heels stepped inside. Without hesitation she strode to the desk. She was a trim, fine-looking person with straight, graying-black hair squeezed into a knob at the back of her head.

A new silence shrouded the room. Again twenty pairs of eyes focused on the teacher. Michael's heart thumped as he watched. He knew that normally his mother was a quiet, soft-spoken person who took her Sandemanian faith seriously. Likewise, he knew his parents made it a habit to side with the teacher. Still, this was a most unusual occasion.

"I've not been a-sendin' my children to this school to be mocked and beaten," she announced crisply. "And since that seems to be yer specialty, I'm a-takin' 'em out of school—"

"I-I-I," sputtered the teacher. Her neck shrunk into the hollow of her thin shoulders as if she were a turtle. "I-I-I—"

"I'm indeed sorry that I'll be a-reducin' yer income," continued Mrs. Faraday. "But with all this inflation we could use the tuition money to buy more food. Two slices of bread a day fer each of us ain't quite enough to keep soul and body together!"

As Michael trailed his mother outside, he snatched a last glance at his teacher. Her face had turned chalky-pale and her eyebrows were so close they resembled an ox-yoke. Michael felt a pinch of guilt at leaving. Deep in his middle he had half-a-thimble of respect for his teacher even though she had never spent a day in preparing for her position. He knew she wasn't any worse than many other teachers in the schools of that time.

The creak of the school door opening whirled the Faradays around before they had gone fifty feet. Michael stared and his jaw sagged.

Framed in the doorway, her black dress drooping to the soles of high, black shoes, stood the teacher. The whiteness in her cheeks had been transferred into splotches of red. "I was only a-doin' me duty," she squeaked. "Unless Michael learns to say *r* he won't amount to no nothin'. There jist ain't no chance fer him, unless he wants to become one of them black-faced chimbly sweeps!" She cocked her head to one side as she contemplated such a life. "Reckon it don't matter much how he talks if he wants to spend his time a-bustin' his bones climbin' the insides of chimblys."

She started to close the door, hesitated, and then in a I'm-sorry-for-you tone, added, "If you ever change your mind, Mrs. Faraday, we'll be glad to take him back."

Mrs. Faraday continued toward home without replying. As the family walked the narrow—and frequently smelly—streets toward Manchester Square, Michael had to force himself to keep up with the determined strides of his mother. In his daydreams he had imagined himself returning home after a day's work and handing his mother a fistful of shillings to help with family expenses. Having heard the lashing words of the teacher, these dreams now seemed impossible. All of them! It was as if Meg had shredded them into bits with her play scissors.

As Michael pondered the meaning of what the teacher had said, a dreadful emptiness gnawed at his stomach. It seemed that he was a hollowed out bit of nothing, that he was utterly worthless. The idea of being a chimney sweep was horrible. Ugh!

He had worked for hours trying to say *rat* instead of *wat*. It was useless. If a flogging would help, he gladly would have submitted. Frustrated, he kicked a heavy stone.

"Don't wear out your shoes," cautioned Mrs. Faraday. "Pa has been sick all week and I don't know when he'll be able to go to work again."

"Wish I could say wabet wight," sobbed Michael, digging knuckles into his eyes. "But I can't. My tongue just won't say it!"

"Don't give up, Michael," she said, squeezing his hand. "Robert will help you, won't you, Robert?"

"Of course."

Michael tried to push the frustration of the impediment from his mind. But while he struggled, other things bothered him. A vivid scene from the week before focused in his mind. "Your noggin is so long it reminds me of a stale loaf of bread," the school bully had taunted. He was a dull, ill-mannered boy of fifteen with a thin nose that jutted from his face like the prow of a slave ship. "They ought to lock you in the zoo with the monkeys. You'd be a sight with a banana in yer paws! Wouldn't he, fellows?"

"That he would," agreed a boy in a tall sweater.

"Maybe that's why he can't say r," reasoned another. "Maybe the sound gets lost in his head."

"My ma told me I shouldn't play with you, that you're a dirty dissenter," said another. "She said you wash one another's feet in your church. My! My! What's the matter Sandy Man? A boy with a bean as long as yours ought to have enough sense to scrub his own feet! Ain't that so?"

"Yeah, that's so," chorused the group.

With such memories tormenting his brain, Michael's spirits flopped to a new low. "Why did I have to be bown?" he sobbed, peering into his mother's face.

"Shh, Michael," rebuked Mrs. Faraday. "Don't talk like that. You were born because God has a purpose fer your life!"

"How do you know?"

"Because He has a purpose for everyone—"

"How can that be?"

"Because the Good Book says so."

"How do you know the Bible is twue?"

"I know it's true because I've proved it."

As they approached the place where they lived in Jacob's Well Mews on the north side of Manchester

Square, Mrs. Faraday cautioned, "Now boys, try and be quiet. Yer pa is very ill. And you, Michael, don't pester him with a lot of questions that only God knows the answer to! Pa has troubles enough without that."

While Robert and his mother mounted the creaky outside steps leading to the family quarters on the second floor, just above the coach house, Michael noted the number of chalk marks on the upstairs door. Then he darted into the lower part of the building where the coaches were parked. He picked up the stubby pencil attached to a string just behind the double doors in the front.

"Home kind of early, aren't you," questioned an elderly worker with a white beard overflowing to his chest.

"Yeah," agreed Michael sadly.

"What's the matter, Master Michael? You sound kind of worried," said the man as he slipped a bit into a horse's mouth.

"I just dwopped out of school. Teacha says I don't talk wight. Guess I'll become a chimbly sweep—"

"Oh, it ain't that bad! Maybe you could become a blacksmith like yer pa. As long as there are horses in London they'll have to be shoed. . . ."

"No, Pa says I ain't stwong enough to do that." He surveyed a row of black marks on the wall and added another with the pencil. He had just finished when Robert stepped through the door.

"Pa wants to see you," said his older brother.

2

THE "R" BARRIER

"Come here, lad," wheezed James Faraday, motioning from his featherbed. After taking Michael's hand in his own, he said, "I'm sorry you had to drop out of school. Still, I think it's fer the best. Some of them schoolteachers don't know much! Besides, you already know how to read and figure all the sums you'll ever need to figure. By a-knowin' how to read you can learn on yer own. Lots of people does. The streets of London are—" He was interrupted by a coughing spell.

He coughed so violently Michael feared he was about to die. "Can I get you something?" he asked a little desperately.

"Naw. I'll be all right. As I was a-sayin' London is an open book. You can git an eddication by just a-lookin' at the street signs." He reached for a glass of water. "Me and Margaret would like to send you to a better school. But Mike, with this sickness and all we ain't got the money. We've apprenticed Robert to a blacksmith. Diggin' up the five pounds to pay the premium took jist 'bout all the savin's we have. We paid for Robert first because he's three years older'n you and he has the strong arm of a blacksmith.

"Smithin' ain't fer you, Mike. You gotta be strong like an ox. But don't worry, lad. Me and Margaret are a-prayin' that God will open the way fer you. And He will. Feel it in me bones.

"But this ain't the reason I called you. I called you because I want you to go to the shop where I work and tell 'em I'm sick and can't be there till Monday."

"While you're a-doin' that," added Mrs. Faraday from the door, I want you to call on Dr. Spence. Tell him to come at once. And to hurry." She turned to leave and then stopped. Fumbling in her apron pocket, she withdrew a handkerchief and untied the knot that was in it. Withdrawing a halfpenny, she said, "This belongs to your teacher; and since the school isn't far from the doctor, you can take it back."

"But, Ma—"

"Yes, take it back. The Faradays are poor. But they're honest. All of 'em!"

"Can I go with him?" asked Elizabeth.

Mrs. Faraday frowned.

"Please!"

"All right, if you promise to get the ironing done when you return."

Just as Michael put his hand on the knob, his mother asked, "Now what are you to do?"

"Tell the fawman at the shop that Pa won't come till

Monday, ask Doc Spence to come immediately, and wetun the halfpenny to the teacha." He took Elizabeth by the arm and scooted down the steps.

"Let's call on Doc fiwst," said Mike. "Then we'll go to school—"

"And don't forget to go to the shop," reminded Liz.

Dr. Spence was trimming roses when Michael approached. "Ma says you'd betta come quick," he panted. "Pa's bad. Coughs all the time."

"I'll be right over," boomed the barrel-shaped man. "Probably needs a good bleedin'." He caressed his drooping moustaches and started for his house.

"Don't forget where we live," called Liz. "It's upstairs in Jacob's Well Mews. Right over the coach-house. . . ."

Michael boldly pushed the school door open and bravely led Liz to the teacher's desk.

"So you've come back and brought along a new student as well," said the teacher, beaming like a cat licking cream from its whiskers.

"No, I ain't comin' back," replied Michael uncomfortably. "And this ain't no new pupil. This is my oldah sistah, Liz. I came back because Ma fo'got to bwing back the ha'penny you gave Wabet. Heah it is." He laid it on the desk.

The teacher held the coin between her fingers and stared. Half to herself, she muttered, "The Sandemanians must be honest people. England would be a better place if we had more like them."

"Can Liz say *r*?" called out the bully from the back of the room.

"Nah, she can't. Don't you know she's Michael's sister. Even a three-legged tomcat can say *r*. But none of the

24

Faradays can!" shouted the boy with the thin nose.

"Yes, I can!" said Liz promptly. "Want to hear me?"

"Of course," yelled several.

"All right, I will." She stood at attention in front of the desk and faced the children.

As every eye watched, she said, "Red Robin, the red river rat, ran right 'round the rabbit's rickety rockin' chair, and rubbed his rosy, rusty, red rump on the rumpled red rug."

A stunned silence followed. Then the whole group— including the bully—leaped to its feet and cheered. "How did you learn all of that?" gasped the teacher, her eyes wide.

"From a friend," said Liz, hanging her head modestly. "I learned it so I could teach Michael to say r. You see, when Michael grows up he's a-gonna be a great man and must speak properly."

As Michael and his sister left, the teacher popped the half-penny into Elizabeth's hand. "That's fer entertainin' us," she said.

Hammers were pounding at Boyd's in Welbeck Street when Michael and Liz entered the side door. "I've stopped to tell you that Pa's sick and won't be a-comin till Monday," said Michael to the foreman.

" 'E's been sick a lot 'asn't 'e?" said the leathery man in broad Cockney. "Too bad, for yer pa's a good man. 'Ope 'e gets well soon. . . ."

"Mind if I show Liz awound a bit?" asked Michael.

"Fine, but keep away from the sparks and 'orses. A round tub of a man got burned on 'is be'ind last week. You should 'ave 'eard 'im 'owl. Sounded like a blinkin' tomcat, 'e did!"

Michael took Liz to the huge set of bellows. "See, the metal spout sticks in the hot coals," he explained, lifting his voice in order to be heard above the noise. "When the bellows is squeezed, it pushes wind into the coals and makes 'em hot."

"But why do they want to heat the horseshoes?" asked Liz. She pointed to a sweat-drenched man who was beating a white-hot shoe.

"Because the shoe is soft when it's hot."

"Why?"

"I-I weally don't know. But I'll ask." Michael motioned to a man who had just dropped finished shoe into a tub of water. "Why do you heat it and then cool it?" he asked.

"Because the heat makes it soft."

"Why?"

"I dunno. It just does. The hotter it gets, the softer it gets. If we made it hot enough it would melt like butter."

"Why?" cut in Liz.

"I dunno." He shrugged and picked up another shoe from the fire.

As Michael led his sister out the door, he said, "No one knows much about anything. But someday I will! Yes, someday I'll find out why the sky's blue, why things fall down instead of up, and even what lightning is all about. Yes, Liz, someday I'll know these things."

"But first you must learn to say *r*."

"That's wight," agreed Michael.

Dr. Spence was just getting ready to bleed Mr. Faraday when Michael and Liz burst through the door.

"Shh," said Mrs. Faraday. "Pa can't stand any noise."

"Doc, could I help you?" offered Michael.

"Will the sight of blood make you sick?" asked the doctor, pulling his left moustache.

"No, why should it?"

"Then you can hold the basin."

As Michael held the basin, Dr. Spence tightened a chord around Mr. Faraday's left arm.

"Why did you do that?" asked Michael.

"So the vein will stand out."

"But why do you want to bleed him?"

"Because that will make him better."

"How?"

"It will quiet him."

Dr. Spence picked up his lancet to cut the vein. "This will hurt a little," he said.

"Why don't you wait until he's asleep befaw you cut it?" asked Michael.

"Because that's impossible."

"Why?"

"Because no one could sleep if he knew he was going to be cut while he's asleep."

"Can't you stop the pain some way?"

"I might give him opium or make him drunk. But even that wouldn't stop the pain completely."

"Maybe somebody will invent something that will make the patient go to sleep while he's being cut," suggested Michael.

"Perhaps. But that will take a long time."

"Why?"

"Because men are stupid. William Harvey didn't even discover the circulation of the blood until 1628—almost two hundred years ago!"

Michael closed his eyes as a thin stream of blood spurted into the basin. Satisfied that he had taken enough, Dr. Spence pressed a wad of bandage over the wound and bound it tightly into place.

"How do you decide how much blood to take?" asked Michael.

"Oh, we learn from experience," answered Spence, patting the top of his chalk-white wig knowingly. "For an ordinary fever I take about eight ounces. Of course I vary the amount from case to case. It takes years of experience to know just the right amount. . . ."

After Spence had packed his tools, he said, "Now keep your father quiet. He'll need a lot of rest." He hesitated, and then smiled. "I'm afraid I'll have to ask for my fee. I wish I could extend credit. But with these high prices and all—" He threw up his hands. "The tax on my wig alone is a full guinea! Things are getting so bad I don't know what will happen next."

After pocketing the money, he rushed to the door. "I have another urgent case to see," he said.

Following a dinner made from a loaf of bread and a few scraps of meat Mrs. Faraday had managed to buy at a bargain price, the family relaxed in the living room. It had been an exciting day. After repeating what had happened, Michael said, "Now I want you to help me make that sound I can't make. I know I must do that befo' I can do anything else."

"I think you can say it," put in Robert. "You've just gotten into a bad habit. When I listen to you, I notice that every once in a while you almost say it. Just now you nearly said *before* correctly. The *r* was a little indistinct. Otherwise—"

"Michael, see if you can say my tongue twister," suggested Liz. "Ready?"

Michael nodded.

Attempting to be as distinct as possible, and even exaggerating a bit, Liz repeated the words she had said at school.

"All wight, I'll twy," agreed Michael. With eyes closed and fists squeezed so tight his knuckles whitened, he said, "Wed Wobin, the wed wiva wat, wan wight—"

At this point he was interrupted. With the exception of his mother, everyone howled with laughter. "Don't make fun of him," she admonished. "After all, he's trying!"

"Let me twy again," said Michael, completely unruffled. "If I keep twyin' I'll succeed. I just know I will."

"It's all in your mind," managed Robert after controlling his laughter. "Liz told me that you spoke the foreman at the shop. Jack is a Cockney—and the Cockneys drop all their h's. Jack would die before he'd say *horse*. To him, it's *'orse*. One day I asked him to spell horse, and do you know what he said?"

"I've no idea," said Michael eagerly.

"He said, 'Haitch ho har hes he spells 'orse.' And so you can see he can say *h* if he wants to! It's the same with you. See if you can howl like a tomcat. You know they go errrrrow—"

"All wight, I'll twy."

Michael tried again. But all he could produce was a wobbly wwwwwow.

Again everyone howled with laughter.

Suddenly Mrs. Faraday clapped a hand over her mouth. "I forgot something!" she exclaimed. "I forgot the moon won't be out tonight and that we should keep a candle burning outside. We were almost fined the last time I forgot—and there have been so many thieves recently—"

"Don't worry, I'll light one," offered Elizabeth.
"We don't have any and we've run out of money," wailed Mrs. Faraday.

"Don't worry," said Robert as calm as a wart. "I've got it all worked out. We'll put the living room candle outside—"

"And how will we get to bed?" scorned Elizabeth.

"You don't need light to sleep!" said Robert.

"What about tomorrow?" asked Mrs. Faraday. "We don't—"

"I'll to to Riebau's place," interrupted Elizabeth, "and get three new candles with the ha'penny the teacher gave me for sayin', Red Robin, the red river rat, ran—"

"Don't say that wretched thing again!" protested Robert, heading for his room.

As Michael knelt by the side of the bed he shared with Robert, he prayed that the Lord would help him speak "pwapaly." He also pleaded that his father would get well "pwovided it is Thy will."

3

ON THE STREETS

Remembering his father had suggested that he could get an education on the streets of the city, Michael decided to walk through them, keep his eyes open—and learn what he could. Likewise, he hoped that while doing this he might find employment. There was always a chance someone might pay him a penny or two for delivering a package.

Puzzled why several streets in the Manchester Square neighborhood were called Mews, he determined to investigate. Again and again he stopped scholarly looking people and inquired. Each time the person shrugged. "Does it really make any difference?" asked one, scowling down at him.

Finally, while visiting in the Charing Cross area, he met a tottering old man. "Please," said Michael, "I live in Jacob's Well Mews, and I'd like to know why it's called Mews."

The old man smiled, baring a row of uneven and missing upper teeth. "You've asked the right man!" he said, beaming with enthusiasm. "Years ago I wrote a book about the streets of London. But—" He peered over the top of his gold-rims. "But why would a lad like you be interested in such things?"

"Because I dwopped out of school and want to know about the city."

"Mmmm. Well, I'll tell you." He thoughtfully washed his hands in the air. "The word *mew* is old. It was used by falconers to describe the way hawks cast their feathers. Thus, one of these gentlemen might say, 'My hawks are mewing.' "

Aiming a thumb at a nearby museum which displayed mechanical devices, he continued, "Now this place used to keep the kings' hawks—and many of the kings had a lot of hawks. As you know, falconry is a rich man's sport. The hawks lived here until 1537.

"During that year, Henry VIII—the one with the wives—had the hawks removed and this place made into stables for his horses. He did this because his stables at Bloomsbury burned. The stables are now gone. Still, the name remains. Because of this, I suspect that they keep horses at Jacob's Well Mews. Right?"

"Wight!"

The old man frowned and scoured his hands again. "The streets of London are a school for those who are interested! But no one is." He sighed, and placed a hand on Michael's shoulder. "Ever heard of Birdcage Walk?"

"I-I don't know."

"Well, you should learn the reason for such a curious

name. Did you ever hear the children sing, 'Ring a-ring a-roses, a pocketful of posies, tishoo, tishoo, we all fall down!'?"

Michael nodded. "We used to join hands and dance awound in a ci'cle and then fall down at the end."

"That song was born during the Great Plague. It described the disease. The victims developed a rosy rash. They did a lot of sneezing. Finally, most of them fell down—dead."

He rubbed his chin. "Everyone tried to stop the plague. No one could. Charles II even filled one street with bird cages. He hoped the flapping of the birds' wings would drive away the disease. His idea didn't work—153,849 people died! But that's the reason that street is called Birdcage Walk.

"The only thing that stopped the plague was the Pudding and Pie fire of 1666—"

"Puddin' and Pie fiah! What's that?" asked Michael, his eyes circles of wonder.

"Well, you see the Great London Fire started in a bakery in Pudding Lane and it didn't stop until it got to Pie Corner. That fire destroyed four fifths of London. Nevertheless, the destruction gave Sir Christopher Wren his great opportunity—"

Fearing an endless story, Michael began to inch away.

"Don't you want to hear the story of St. Paul's and Stinking Lane and Bladder Street and Amen Lane?"

"I'd love to, but I-I ain't got time wight now."

The old man motioned him closer. Placing a hand on each shoulder, he said, "I don't know your name. Yet I can see you have a bright mind. This is wonderful. But you must learn to speak correct English. Never say *ain't*. That word is like a dead fly in a pudding. Also, you should say right instead of wight."

"I want to say w-w-wight wight. But I can't. Could you help me?"

You could learn. I'm a cockney and I used to say 'orse. Now I can say *horse*." He scrubbed his hands in the air again. "Have you ever noticed the position of your tongue when you say certain letters?"

"Can't say that I have."

"Try it sometime. It might help." With that, he glanced at his pocket watch and headed in the direction of Pall Mall.

Three weeks after this, Michael was strolling by some high-chimneyed houses when he heard a man in a stove-pipe hat shouting, "Sweep! Sweep!" Noticing Michael, he crossed the street.

"Chimbly sweepin' is a fine business," he said. "Why don't you go to work fer me? Pay's good and when you learn the business ya' can wear a stovepipe hat and hire others."

"We don't have the pwemium," replied Michael, stepping closer.

"Who said anything about a premium?" asked the man. "I wouldn't take a premium even if you offered it. Instead, I'll pay a premium to your parents."

"Weally?"

"Sure!" He pulled two one-pound notes from his pocket and waved them in front of Michael.

Michael was so startled he was speechless.

"All right, then, I'll pay three pounds, but narry a penny more."

Thinking about the things so much money could buy—medicine for his father, food for the table, and repairs for the stove—Michael couldn't have uttered a sound even if he'd been stuck by a pin.

"You're a great bargainer," said the sweep. "Ain't seen none like you for a long time! So, I'll tell you what I'll do. I'll give you five pounds. And that's a lot of money. Of course we'd have to go to the magistrate and make it all legal, ya' know."

"I'll think about it," said Michael eagerly.

As Michael hurried home, he felt as if he was walking on air. Five pounds! That much money would give his family such a boost everything would be changed. Perhaps it would even help his father get well. Of course, the apprenticeship would be for perhaps seven years and during that time he'd be legally bound to the sweeper. Still—

Michael was passing an enormous Elizabethan house when he noticed a series of carts outside. Each cart was overloaded with dirty bags of soot. Since the front doors to the large brick dwelling were open, he cautiously climbed the steps and peaked inside.

"You're just what we need!" boomed a well-dressed man in a white waistcoat. "I'm getting another chimney cleaned and we need some help to shift the furniture."

After the rugs and tables had been moved out of the living room, Michael asked if he could remain and watch.

"Stay if you like," replied the man, pressing a shilling into his hand.

Presently a tiny lad whose head had been shaved until it was as smooth as an egg took a brush and started up the chimney. "Now hurry!" snapped the manager, a squat man with a broken stovepipe hat on his head. "And no foxin'! We've got two more jobs today."

"What do you mean, 'no foxin'?" asked Michael, frowning.

The hatted man shrugged. "Oh, some of these lazy brats find a place where the chimney branches out. Then they lie down in the flat place and rest. Some of 'em even go to sleep!"

"What do you do if he wests?" asked Michael.

"If he's close enough I poke him with a wire. When that doesn't work I burn a couple of straws at the bottom of the chimbly. Nothin' works better'n that. Yeah, a little fire makes 'em scoot!"

Soon streams of soot began to fill the fireplace and billow out into the room. "Ain't you afwaid he'll suffocate?" asked Michael, his eyes wide with alarm.

"Some of 'em do. Some of 'em even bust their legs and lose their sight; and that soot's pi'zen in their lungs. Makes 'em cough all the time. But what else can a boy of seven do for a livin'?"

"You mean he's only seven?" gasped Michael. "By the looks of him I'd think he was at least twelve."

"That's right. He's only seven. This kind of work ages a kid. He's been workin' for me since he was six. His pa's dead, and his ma ain't no good." Suddenly he stopped and his eyes turned cold. "But say, who are you anyway? You sound like that umbrella man!"°

"Was just a-thinkin' of becomin' a sweep myself," confessed Michael. "A man just told me that it's a good business."

"Don't do it!" He removed his hat and wiped his

°Jonas Hanway, inventor of the umbrella, started an agitation against the use of children as chimney sweeps in 1773. The practice was not outlawed until 1875.

brow. "This ain't no business for a gentleman." As he spoke, the sweep stepped out of the fireplace. The boy was saturated with soot from the top of his head to the soles of his feet, and Michael noticed that his arms and legs were deformed. Probably this was a result of spending so much time in such narrow places during his growing years, Michael decided.

"I'd better slide down from the top," said the lad.

The moment the boy stepped through the door, the manager said, "And now you can see why so many sweeps stay drunk half the time. They can't go to school and they have no time to play. They're just like animals. A penny's worth of gin helps 'em forget they're troubles—for a few hours."

After Michael had finished relating the happenings of the day, his mother said, "I've been a-prayin' that God will guide you. And I think He has. Lots of chimbly sweeps could have done better if they'd a-listened to the heavenly Father. Some might even have made it to Parliament. God wants the best for His children! . . ."

"Yes, but think of what Pa could have done with the five pounds!"

"Oh, laddie, money ain't everything. Happiness don't come from things. Happiness comes from within."

All at once the door burst open and Liz zoomed into the room. "Guess what! Guess what!" she shouted.

"What?" asked Michael and his mother together.

"I got a job for Michael! I got a job for—"

"Y-you got a job for me?" exclaimed Michael.

"Yes, I got a job for you with Monsieur George Riebau at No. 2 Blandford Street."

"You mean the refugee bookbinder?" asked Mrs. Faraday.

"Yes," replied Elizabeth, nodding her head vigorously. "Of course he don't want to teach him to bind books yet. But—"

"You mean he might teach me the twade?" asked Michael, his eyes shining.

"That's right, he just might. And the best part is that Blandford Street is very close. All you have to do is to go two blocks west on Charles and one block north on Baker. And do you know why he wants to hire you?"

"Why?"

"Because when I bought the candles from Monsieur Riebau I told him how Michael had to return the ha'penny to the teacher. He told me that he had never heard of such honesty in his whole life. That's why he wants Michael to work for him!"

"This has been a good day," rejoiced Mrs. Faraday. 'Pa has gone to work, Michael has escaped becomin' a chimbly sweep, and we're a-gonna have meat fer supper—"

"And I was paid a shillin'," cut in Michael as he placed it on the table.

"For all of this, we ought to thank the Lord," concluded Mrs. Faraday, kneeling at her chair.

As the family lounged in the living room, Michael told them how the old man had taught him the meaning of the word "mew."

"What's the difference what it means?" demanded Elizabeth.

"It makes a lot of diffwence," replied Michael heatedly. "I believe we should get to the bottom of things. Besides, nothin' excites me so much as lea'nin' somethin' new."

"You'd be better off if you learned to say *r*."

Suddenly Michael was on his feet. "That old man gave me an idea!" he exclaimed. "Liz, sit hewe by the candle."

"Why should I do that?" she asked, going toward it.

After Liz had reluctantly seated herself, Michael said, "Now open yo' mouth—wide; and while it's still open let me watch yo' tongue while you say the alphabet."

"Are you crazy, or have you decided to become a dentist?" she demanded, her mouth sagging.

"Neithah. I-I just w-want to twy somethin'."

Holding the candle close to his big sister's mouth, Michael said, "Now say *a*."

As Liz complied, Michael noted, "When you say *a*, the tip of yo' tongue was wight at the bottom of yo' fwont teeth. Now say *b*."

This time he observed that the tip of her tongue was slightly behind where it had been when she said *a*.

After trying several letters, he said, "Now Liz, say that letta I can't say."

"Rrrrr."

"Now say it the way I say it."

"Wwwwww."

"Now say it one way and then the othah," said Michael, his voice bright with excitement.

As Liz complied, Michael held the candle so close he almost burned her. "Don't set me on fire," she said, pushing away his hand.

"Sowwy. But do just as I said."

"Ah, I'm beginnin' to see," he almost shouted. "When you say it the wight way yo' tongue is at the top of yo' mouth and when you say it the wong way yo' tongue is at the bottom of yo' mouth. Now let me sit while you watch my tongue."

After changing places, Elizabeth said, "Say rat."

"Wat," replied Michael.

"Now make your tongue go to the roof of your mouth while you say rat," she coached. As she spoke, the entire family came close to observe.

"Don't suff-o-cate me!" pleaded Michael, pretending he was gasping for breath.

After the family had inched back, he closed his eyes and clenched his fists. This was *the* test! If he failed, he might not succeed at anything. For a moment his mind went back to the chimney sweep. He saw his shaved head, twisted arms and legs, and remembered the pathetic look in his swollen eyes. He even smelled the swirling soot. Then he seemed to hear his teacher's words as she spoke from the door of the school: "Unless Michael learns to say *r* he won't amount to nothin'. There jist ain't no chance fer him, unless he wants to become one of them black-faced chimbly sweeps!" Tantalized by these memories, he made a supreme effort.

"W-w-w-w-r-at," he managed.

"You almost said it! You almost said it!" cried Liz with such enthusiasm she nearly blew out the candle. "Now relax and try again."

"W-rat, w-rat, rat," said Michael, his hands open, but his eyes wide.

"Now say Robert."

"W-w-w-w-robert. W-robert. Robert!" he said.

"Now growl like a tomcat," said Robert, cutting in.

"Errrrrow."

Realizing he had succeeded, Michael leaped to his feet, lifted Meg to his hip, and danced a jig. "You're going to put the candle out!" shouted Elizabeth, snatching it away and fixing it in a holder.

"I'm sowwy! I mean I'm sorry!" exclaimed Michael on the verge of tears. "But this is the happiest day in my life! Robert! Robert! Robert! Errrrrrrow. Errrrrrrow. Errrrrrrrow!"

"I'm happy fer you," said James Faraday. After flinging an arm around Michael's shoulders and squeezing him until he groaned, he added, "You've learned to conquer a problem by getting to the roots. Havin' learned that, you'll conquer other problems. . . . To succeed, a person has to get to the roots. Michael, you've got determination. That's what it takes!"

Suddenly Michael's face fell. "I forgot to make my mark downstairs," he wailed.

"That's all right," said Liz cheerfully. "I knew you'd forget and so I did it fer you!"

4

ERRAND BOY

Michael squirmed as his mother adjusted his home-made hat. "I want you to look jist right," she explained, stepping back and viewing him proudly. "Hope Monsieur Riebau likes yer work. I've heard—" She thoughtfully bit her lip. "I've heard he's very particular. Pa and me will be a-prayin' fer you!"

The entire downstairs of No. 2 Blandford Street was fronted by three large windows and each window was divided into sets of oblong panes. Pictures, together with boxes of stationary and stacks of books, were neatly arranged behind most of the panes. A table loaded with books stood outside and nearby was a row of upended newspapers. The Riebau apartment was above the store.

"Your first job will be to deliver newspapers," said Riebau. He spoke with just a trace of a Parisian accent.

He was a round-faced, olive-skinned man with a drooping white moustache and a receding hairline of straight, matching hair. "Now these newspapers are not being sold. Rather, we merely rent them out for three or four hours—" He glanced at the clock. "This means you must be quite punctual—even in bad weather."

"Wenting—I-I mean renting newspapers?" stammered Michael, his eyes widening.

"Yes, yes, I rent them. There's a tax on papers when people buy them. But there's no tax when they're rented!" He closed his right eye and nodded knowingly. Next he pointed to a pile of papers and handed Michael a long list of addresses. "Deliver these right now. Then this afternoon you will go around and pick them up—and collect the rental money.

"It will take a while to deliver them at first. In time it will be routine. Still, you must be accurate. Also, take care not to be robbed. This is a dangerous neighborhood."

Michael already knew most of the streets where the papers were to be delivered. His greatest problem was in collecting the papers on time—and in getting the money. Often as he asked for the paper the man of the house replied, "We need more time. . . ."

While waiting for one customer to finish, Michael stuck his head between the bars of the iron barrier that divided one house from the other. When he tried to jerk his head out, he found he was stuck.

Considering that his head was on one side and his body on the other side, he questioned which side he—the real he—was on. This mental game didn't last, for when in twisting to get his head out, he accidentally bloodied his nose. The sight of blood pushed the question from his mind.

It was 1803—an exciting year. Napoleon Bonaparte had broken the Peace of Amiens by declaring war on England. In his effort to break "the nation of shopkeepers" (the sneering title Napoleon gave the English) he stationed formidable armies on the coast of France directly across from England. But the dreaded conqueror of large sections of Europe hesitated to attack because Britain controlled the seas.

In this tense atmosphere, with the masses fearing invasion any minute, English newspapers were dominated by headlines—and Michael's customers wanted their papers promptly. Years before, English journalists had ridiculed Napoleon. They referred to him as "Puss in Boots" because of his high boots. Now, with unbelievable success behind him, they quivered with respect. Even flimsy stories made splashes in the papers.

One headline screamed: *French Plan Tunnel Under Channel!* Another: *Boney Is Waiting for Long Winter Nights Before Attack.*

When Thomas Jefferson concluded the Louisiana Purchase on April 30, 1803, for fifteen million dollars, England was gravely concerned. Michael's paper declared: *Boney Has New Funds For Armaments.*

Michael was not interested in the war. But sometimes he had to read the stories to illiterate customers. About the only ones who didn't discuss the war were the Quakers and Anabaptists.

"If your paper doesn't stop printing so many things about the war, we're going to stop taking it," threatened an Anabaptist.

"Why do you say that?" inquired Michael, noticing the man's unusually plain garments.

"Because we're against all violence."

During the long conversation, Michael learned that there were thirty-three Anabaptist congregations in London and that they had such intriguing names as Angel Alley Meeting, Whitechapel; and Goat Yard Passage, Horselydown.

"Where do you attend?" asked Michael.

"Oh, I'm a member of the Glasshouse Yard Meeting, Pickaxe Street. Unusual name, yes?"

"It's not only unusual but interesting," agreed Michael.

After the papers were returned, Michael was given other errands to run. One evening Riebau handed him a newly bound set of Sam Johnson's *Dictionary*. "Take these to Mr. Dance," he said. "Here's the address."

Having delivered the heavy package, Michael started to leave.

"Not so fast!" interjected Dance. He was tall and well-groomed. "I often see you at Riebau's. He speaks well of you. What are your plans?"

"I-I really don't know," sputtered Michael, his eyes on the expensive carpet.

Dance carefully opened the package and arranged the books on the table. "My they're beautiful!" he cried. "Just look at that gold lettering. Riebau is not just a bookbinder. He's an artist! Michael, you should persuade him to teach you the trade."

"You mean, become an apprentice?"

"Why not?"

Michael shifted his feet nervously.

"Well, why not?" persisted Dance.

"Because we wouldn't have the premium," said Michael, bluntly.

"Mmmmm, I see," replied Dance thoughtfully.

45

Encouraged by this friendliness, Michael said, "Please, sir, what is the purpose of a dictionary?"

"Oh, it's to give the correct spelling and meaning of words. Sam Johnson's *Dictionary* is one of the best, although it is a little biased—and sometimes humorous." He opened the volume containing *O*. "See, here's his definition of oats. He says it is 'a grain which in England is generally given to horses, but in Scotland supports the people.'"

Michael frowned. "We eat oats and we're not from Scotland."

"Johnson didn't say that no one in England eats oats—"

"Does he say anything about Anabaptists?" asked Michael.

Thumbing through the No. 1 volume, Dance came to the right page. "Ah, here it is. Johnson says that an Anabaptist is 'such an one who alloweth of, and maintaineth rebaptizing.'"

"He's right!" exclaimed Michael. "I just talked to an Anabaptist and he told me that they believe Christian baptism is for believers only. Since infants cannot believe, they rebaptize them when they are old enough to confess Christ and promise to live the rest of their lives for Him.

"A dictionary is a wonderful thing! Can you look up anything in a dictionary?"

"Almost—"

"Could you look up the meaning of the word *mew*?"

As Dance looked up the word, Michael explained how he had met the old man at Charing Cross and what he had said.

With a finger near the reference, Dance read: " 'The word *mue* denotes a change; hence any casting of the coat or skin, as the muing of a hawk.' "

Dance cleared his throat. "And here's more to his definition," he added. "It is, 'A cage for hawks. The king's mews at Charing Cross is the place where formerly the king's hawks were kept.' "

"That's just about what that old man said!" cried Michael excitedly. "But doesn't it say anything about horses?"

"Nothing. You see, language changes—and knowledge grows. Johnson shows that at first this word was spelled *mue*. Later on, he spells it *mew*—just as we spell it today."

"Is Sam Johnson always right?"

"Not always."

"How can you tell?"

"By comparing his dictionary with other dictionaries and encyclopedias."

"What's an encyclopedia?" asked Michael, his eyes almost riveted to those of Mr. Dance.

"An encyclopedia is like a dictionary but it is much larger. Come. I'll show you mine." He led him into his study and pointed to a set of *Britannica.*

"Y-you mean all those books are full of knowledge?" asked Michael. He nervously touched one.

"Yes, of course. And besides encyclopedias there are many other books. Here is a book by Sir Isaac Newton in which he describes the laws of gravity." He handed the book to Michael.

After Michael had glanced through the slender volume, he shook his head. "There are too many big words," he said. "But maybe if I had a dictionary I could look them up and learn their meaning—" He was interrupted by the chiming of the hall clock. "Oh, I must hurry," he said briskly. "Monsieur Riebau will think I'm lost!"

The September of 1805 was a damp one. Heavy fogs squeezed into London. Some were so thick Michael found it difficult to see the homes of customers until he was directly in front of them. But the Faradays were happy. Robert was learning his trade, Michael was so accustomed to his route he had time for two or three games of marbles each week, and Mr. Faraday was well enough to keep working.

During the last Sunday of that month, a bright sun lit the streets around Manchester Square. "It's such a lovely day," rejoiced Mrs. Faraday, "we ought to go to church early. That way we can see the sights. Let's go together as a family."

"I'll have to deliver my papers first," Michael said. He started a little earlier with his papers and walked faster than usual. Upon his return, as he wolfed his breakfast, his father said, "Well, Michael, you're the one who's worked today, and so you can choose the route."

The Sandemanian meetinghouse the Faradays attended was about two and a half miles almost directly east of them. It stood in St. Paul's Alley—a narrow, neglected place that branched from Red Cross Street.

Thinking about which would be the most interesting way, Michael said, "Let's go east on Oxford Street and then north on Aldersgate."

"That's out of the way," objected Elizabeth. "And besides, Oxford Street doesn't go that far!"

"Your father said Michael could choose the way," Mrs. Faraday reminded Elizabeth. "Everyone knows that Oxford Street goes all the way to Aldersgate. It just changes its name on the way like you'll do when you get married. First it becomes High Street, and then Broad Street, and then High Holborn. After that it's Holborn Hill, and then—"

"And then Skinner," interrupted Elizabeth sarcastically.

"Next Skinner becomes Newgate and Newgate becomes Cheapside," concluded Michael. "I have a customer who lives near where the name changes. He's a Jew with whiskers a yard long. But we don't go down Cheapside. Instead, we turn north at Aldersgate."

"Let's stop arguing," said Mr. Faraday warmly. "You know the rule in Sandemanian churches that if there's any disharmony in the congregation no one can partake of the Lord's Supper."

As the family turned north on Aldersgate, Michael passed two-year-old Meg over to Elizabeth. "It's your turn to carry her," he said.

"Aldersgate is a famous street. Why?" asked James Faraday.

"Because it was here that John Wesley became a born again Christian," said Michael.

"That's right," answered his father proudly, for he considered it his solemn duty to teach the family the history of the Sandemanians. "John Wesley is especially important to us. Why?"

"Both John and Charles Wesley are important to us because Benjamin Ingham, one of our founders, was their friend and went with them to Georgia on their missionary trip. And besides, all three of them were members of the Holy Club of Oxford."

"Ah, you are doing well," said Faraday. "Now how do Sandemanians differ from other Christians?"

"We don't believe in state churches. Our belief is in complete separation. That's the reason our founders disagreed with the Wesleys, for the Wesleys continued as members of the Church of England—"

"And how does John Glas fit into the picture?" persisted Faraday.

"Glas was a minister in the Presbyterian Church—the state church of Scotland. When he was convinced that the Word does not even mention a state church, he began to preach separation. As a result, the elders put him out in 1730. He then founded a congregation in Dundee."

"True. But why are we not called Glasites?"

"We *were* in the beginning," said Michael, proud of his knowledge. "Then Robert Sandeman came along. He married the daughter of Glas and wrote books filled with our doctrine. Because of Sandeman's books we are called Sandemanians. That sounds like a strange sect, but really we're just simple Christians who take the Bible seriously."

"I thought we were out to enjoy a pleasant walk," grumbled Elizabeth after she had passed Meg over to Robert. "Instead, we're having a class in church history!" As she spoke, a fine carriage drawn by four white horses almost splashed water on them.

"These facts are most important," said Mr. Faraday, unaware of the near-accident. "It's my duty to make certain you know them!"

As the family turned east from Aldersgate into St. Paul's Alley, they entered one of the worst slums of the city. The street was jammed with rickety tenement houses overflowing with some of London's poorest people. Broken windows—many patched with filthy rags—

gaped into the street. Twisted webs of clotheslines, sagging with patched clothes, snaked in all directions.

The Faradays were not distracted by the filthy street, the flea-bitten dogs, or even the drunks stretched on the walks or angled on the steps. Instead, their eager eyes sought out the well-kept, well-scrubbed meetinghouse. They approached it with the same enthusiasm that a thirsty man approaches an oasis.

The Faradays had attended this congregation from the time they had moved to London. Even James Faraday's parents had been members. To them, the extremely plain building was a place of refuge. It was their castle—their second home.

As the family ascended the steps and entered the building, they exchanged affectionate "kisses of peace" with other brothers and sisters. The Sandemanians did not believe in a paid clergy. Instead, the preaching and administration was done by untrained elders—some almost illiterate. The Bible—as interpreted by Robert Sandeman—was their sole authority.

Following the morning services, the Faradays, as was the custom, joined the others in a separate room for their midday meal. At the conclusion of the five o'clock service, a collection was received for the poor. Next, the faithful filed into a separate room to partake of the Lord's Supper.

The congregation also practiced foot washing. They insisted that Jesus had introduced this custom in the Upper Room, and that He commanded His followers to continue the practice down through the centuries.

As Michael was leaving the shop one Saturday night in early October, Monsieur Riebau summoned him into the back room. After closing the door, he said, "Madam and I have been watching you for a long time and we've come to an agreement." He fidgeted with his moustache.

"As you know, we have no children. We've wondered if you'd like to become an apprentice."

"And learn bookbinding?" exclaimed Michael, trying to keep the excitement out of his voice.

"Of course."

"I'd love to, but—"

"But what?"

"I-I-I'm afraid we don't have the premium."

"Nonsense. Did I say anything about a premium?"

"Y-you mean I can sign up without a premium?" asked Michael, unable to believe his ears.

"That's what I said. But first I want you to check with your parents. Also, you'd better pray about it!"

As Michael went home that evening, it was all he could do to keep from running.

5

FROG LEGS

"Bookbindin' is a mighty good trade!" said Mr. Faraday. He spoke from the bed where he had been confined for three days by his old sickness. "You won't have to do a lot of standin' and you won't have to fiddle with no fire—" He grew tense and began to cough into a red handkerchief.

"But me and Ma will be a-missin' you. Still, Blandford Street ain't far—" He coughed again. "I still can't believe that there's no premium—"

"It's the hand of the Lord!" Mrs. Faraday commented enthusiastically from her chair at the foot of the bed.

While Michael was visiting with his parents, Liz breezed in. "Don't worry about the marks downstairs," she said, standing close to Michael. "I'll make 'em for you!"

Mrs. Faraday cocked her head to one side. "What's the purpose of them marks?" she inquired.

"They're just to keep a check on the milkman," said Michael. "Some of these milkmen put an extra chalk mark on the door when the women aren't watchin'. So far, our man has been honest. And yet—"

"But why did you make the marks downstairs?"

"Because me and Liz like to be mysterious!"

On October 7, 1805, Mr. Faraday went with Michael to sign the legal papers with George Riebau. Included in the printed document binding Michael to serve seven years as an apprentice were a number of stern sentences. One forbad him to "play cards, dice, or any other unlawful games." Another insisted that he was not to "frequent taverns, alehouses, and tippling houses." Likewise, he was forbidden to marry during his apprenticeship.

Michael smiled at these requirements. None cramped him in any way. How could they? He was only fourteen!

The formal line which had a space to indicate the amount of premium paid, had been crossed out. On top was written, "In consideration of his faithful service no premium is given."

Before signing, James Faraday had a question. "Will Michael be permitted to attend our church on Sundays?"

"Certainly."

Assured, both Michael and his father signed.

The next day Michael hunched in a space beneath a large window as he began his training. He learned that books are made up of numerous sections called *signatures*. Riebau taught him how to glue these signatures together by their spines. Often as he worked, he marveled at the artistic way in which Riebau handled the books. The master never wasted a movement.

"You work with books as if you were handling jewels," laughed Michael.

"And that's what they are," replied Riebau, massaging his moustache. "There's enough knowledge in the books in this room to change the world! Trouble is the owners don't take time to read them. Too many just keep books for show. Incidentally, I want you to feel free to read any of the books in this shop."

"Thanks," replied Michael sheepishly. "But I've already started doing just that. I read Defoe's *Robinson Crusoe* last week. It was so interesting I couldn't put it down."

During the first week of November, London suddenly exploded with joy. The streets blackened with crowds. Bands played. Soldiers marched. And newsboys shouted, "Extra! Extra!"

Michael learned that on October 21 Lord Nelson had defeated a combination of French and Spanish ships at Trafalgar near the southern coast of Spain. He also heard that Nelson had been killed in the battle and that his body was being preserved in a barrel of whisky.

Michael was thankful that there was no longer a possibility that Napoleon would invade England. But his main interest remained in the books he was binding. His great hope was that he could read every one of them.

As preparation were being made for Nelson's funeral on January 9, 1806, an excited customer barged into the shop. Having paid for his stationary, he began a detailed discussion of the famous naval battle. With a quick pencil he sketched the position of the ships. Michael watched and listened. But he was not really interested.

Noticing Michael's lack of concern, the customer asked, "What is it about the whole affair that interests you most?"

"There are only two main things in that affair that really interest me," said Michael. "The first is, Why did it take almost two weeks for the news of the battle to reach England? And the second is, Why did they put Nelson's body in a barrel of whisky?"

"The answers are easy," replied the man, puffing out his chest. "The news of the battle was delayed because of a storm; and Lord Nelson's body was put into the barrel of spirits in order to preserve it."

"I understand all of that," replied Michael. "But I'm interested in knowing how alcohol can preserve a human body for three months; and also why a message could not be sent from one place to another at the speed of light. After all, Olaus Roemer, the Danish astronomer, has shown that light travels at a speed of 192,000 miles per second."°

"You want to know too much," said the man as he headed for the door.

"Perhaps!" replied Michael.

Michael enjoyed his work. Having unusually agile fingers, strengthened by years of playing marbles, he found it easy to manipulate the tools of his trade. In later years, he boasted that "he could strike 1,000 blows with the mallet in succession without resting."

Michael read all of the books available and the time

°He came to this conclusion by a calculation based on the moons of Jupiter. Today we know that the correct speed of light is 186,272 miles per second.

slipped by quickly. In 1809, four years after he had started his apprenticeship, his father wrote about him to a friend. "Michael is a bookbinder and a stationer, and is very active at learning his business. He has been most part of four years of his time out of seven. He has a very good master and mistress, and likes his place well. He had a hard time for some while at first going; but, as the old saying goes, he has rather got the head above water, as there is (sic) two other boys under him."

One afternoon Michael happened to notice that a threadbare set of the *Encyclopedia Britannica* had been brought in to be bound. Remembering the set he had seen at the home of Mr. Dance, he eagerly pulled out a volume to see what he could find. By a startling chance his eyes fell on an article on electricity by James Tytler— a chemist.

The article was profusely illustrated with drawings of electrical experiments performed in the preceding century. Almost hypnotized by what he read, he had to force himself to close the books and stay with his work.

Day after day as Michael reached for the glue, cut the tapes, pounded with the mallet, and did the dozens of other things that were necessary to complete a book, his mind was on those articles in the *Britannica*. From them he learned that the word electricity had evolved from the Greek word for amber—*elektron.* He also discovered that many centuries before Christ the Greeks knew that if a piece of amber is vigorously rubbed on a wool cloth it will both attract and repel tiny bits of paper.

Intrigued, Michael determined to perform an experiment and thus prove to himself whether or not these articles in *Britannica* were true. But first he would have to find a piece of amber!

Amber, he learned, is a yellowish substance formed in prehistoric times out of the resin or sap of pine trees that grew in Northern Europe. It had come into being in much the same way as coal was formed. Furthermore, he found that fine quality amber had been used by Greeks to manufacture jewelry. Poorer grades, even in his time, he learned, were used in creating varnish.

Fortunately, Riebau had a small slab of the stuff. While alone in his room, Michael shredded a corner of newspaper into tiny pieces. Then he rubbed the amber on the seat of his pants. Next, he cautiously brought the amber close to the paper. He had strong doubts that anything would happen. Indeed, the whole idea seemed ridiculous and he felt rather foolish.

Nevertheless, as the amber drew closer and even closer to the paper, the tiny bits seemed to come to life. First they stood on end. Then almost invisible fibers stretched out like whiskers. Michael's mouth fell open in awe as he watched. He kept pushing the amber closer. And then it happened. Tiny bits of paper leaped through the air and clung to the amber.

Like a tight spring suddenly released, Michael erupted out of his chair. "It works! It works!" he shouted, dancing up and down.

Suddenly the door opened and Madam Riebau stepped inside. "What works?" she demanded, her dark eyes slanting at him curiously.

"The amber and the paper! Look, I'll show you what happens."

After the demonstration, the plump woman threw an arm around him and scratched his head affectionately. "You're quite a boy!" she exclaimed. "But Michael, you shouldn't rub amber on the seat of your Sunday pants!"

She paused and thoughtfully bit her lip. "I have some old patches I'll let you have."

Ecstatic with the joy of discovery, Michael performed other experiments. He rubbed the amber in various ways and for different lengths of time before he used it. He also rubbed other things. To his satisfaction he discovered that his rubber comb worked as well as amber. Mystified by the phenomenon, he read all he could find on the subject.

In one of the books he had borrowed from a friend, he read that 600 years before Christ, the astronomer Thales of Miletus, noted as one of the Seven Wise Men of Ancient Greece, had tried to explain the action of rubbed amber on paper by suggesting that amber had a "soul" that "sucked" up the paper. Michael frowned at this idea, for it obviously contradicted the Bible which teaches that only humans have a soul. Still, he was intrigued. "I'm going to learn all that can be learned about electricity," he vowed.

By keeping his candles burning late, Michael delved into the mysteries of the compass, the loadstone, the Leyden jar—and especially the discoveries of Benjamin Franklin. This Yankee master of all trades had made startling experiments and discoveries in the late 1740s and early 1750s. Also, he had written some curious observations which had produced amazing results—even in other countries. Michael was almost breathless as he read one set of observations, for they totally agreed with his own.

Dating his observation, November 7, 1749, Franklin wrote: "Electrical fluid agrees with lightning in these particulars. 1. Giving light. 2. Color of the light. 3. Crooked direction. 4. Swift motion. 5. Being conducted by metals. 6. Crack or noise in exploding. 7. Subsisting in water or ice. 8. Rending bodies it passes through. 9. Destroying animals. 10. Melting metals. 11. Firing inflamable substances. 12. Sulphureous smell. The electric fluid is attracted by points. We do not know whether this property is in lightning. But since they agree in all particulars wherein we can already compare them, is it not probable they agree likewise in this? Let the experiment by made."

Franklin then suggested what has come to be known as the lightning rod. He wrote: "I am of the opinion that houses, ships, and even towers and churches may be effectually secured from the strokes of lightning. . . ." His suggestion was that "a rod of iron eight or ten feet in length, sharpened gradually to a point like a needle, and gilt to prevent rusting, or dividing into a number of points" be placed on the tops of churches, spires, and masts. Next, he predicted, "the electrical fire [will], I think, be drawn out of a cloud silently before it [can] come near enough to strike. . . ."

As Michael read this, he noted that Franklin had said nothing about a ground wire. Perhaps, reasoned Michael, the great American did not know that this was necessary. At least not at the time he composed the suggestion. Such a possibility exhilarated him, for even he, an apprenticed bookbinder, knew that a lightning rod was not safe unless it was thoroughly grounded—and so did the fashionable women of the period. This was obvious, for those who peaked their hats with lightning rods also made it a point to trail an adequate ground wire!

Pigeonholing lightning rods and the nature of electricity for a time, Michael switched his attention to magnetism and loadstones. Again, he was spellbound.

He learned that the first loadstone—a chunk of magnetic iron the size of a man's head—had been found at a distant and forgotten date in a country of Asia Minor called Magnesia.

According to legend, a shepherd was attracted to this unusual stone because it grabbed the iron end of his staff. Hundreds of years after its discovery, Europeans discovered that if this stone, or just a piece of it, was suspended by a string it always pointed to the north. Because of this characteristic, they called it a "leading stone." Soon, leading stone became loadstone. *

Following this change of names, it became popular to refer to a loadstone as a *magnesian stone*. Again the name was shortened, and from the new versions we have the words: *magnetite, magnetism,* and *magnet*.

In time, this stone was used to develop the compass. Since the compass enabled sailors to navigate without the use of stars, the loadstone was highly valued. A medieval law decreed that any seaman caught tampering with the ship's loadstone "shall, if his life be spared, be punished by having the hand which he most uses, fastened by a dagger or knife thrust through it, to the mast or principal timber of the ship. . . ."

Having learned that Benjamin Franklin and others had identified electricity with lightning through their famous kite experiments, Michael began to wonder if magnetism could also be identified with electricity. He knew that this was a wild thought. Nevertheless, if magnetism could be transferred from a loadstone to the needle of a compass it must be some kind of a fluid.

---

* Loadstones are still mined. The main sources are Siberia, the Island of Elba, and Arkansas.

Could it be that these fluids are the same?

Michael's thoughts centered around these things until his imagination was suddenly gripped by the reports of a recent argument between a pair of Italian professors that had amused all of Europe. While Luigi Galvani was lecturing on anatomy at the Unversity of Bologna, he chanced to be dissecting a frog when an assistant produced a spark with a static-electric machine in the same room. The moment the spark snapped, the frog's legs twitched.

Astounded by such a reaction, Galvani began to experiment. During a thunderstorm, he attached the frog's legs to a brass hook and suspended the hook over an iron fence. As the wind from the storm blew, the legs occasionally touched the fence. Each time they did, they twitched violently.

Following this experiment, he placed a frog's leg on a board. Next, he touched the nerve in the leg with a zinc rod and the muscle with a copper rod. Nothing happened until he touched the ends of the rods together. When that contact was made, the leg twitched. Intrigued, Galvani tended to overlook the fact that the leg did not twitch unless he used two different types of metal. Soon he was all but convinced that he had discovered the much sought "lifeforce"!

In 1791 Galvani boldly published the idea that he had discovered "animal electricity." °

At first, Professor Volta believed that his friend Gal-

°Galvani was proved wrong by the measurements of his and the next century. Today, however, with our extremely sensitive measuring devises, we know that animals do produce electricity. Galvani's name is reflected in such modern words as *galvanism* and *galvanic current*.

vani was right. Soon, however, he had doubts. Being a physicist, he began to suspect that instead of the leg producing electricity, it had twitched because it had been touched by an outside source of electricity. This electricity, he reasoned, was produced by the contact between two different metals.

Volta's new theory canceled the *animal electricity* and *lifeforce* theory of Galvani. It also sent shock waves through the intellectuals of the time. Volta now realized that he would have to demonstrate publicly that he was right. Feverishly, he assembled apparatus and went to work.

By 1796, this son of a former Jesuit priest had developed what is now known as the *voltaic pile*. This he did by putting a brine-soaked piece of felt on top of a coin-sized copper plate, then placing a same-sized disk of zinc on top of this—thus forming a sandwich. After piling various numbers of these sandwiches on top of each other, he connected a wire to the lowest copper plate and another wire to the zinc on the highest plate.

When these two wires were touched together a spark was produced. Moreover, he found that such a spark could be produced again and again. In this way, the pile differed from the Leyden jar which produced only a spark or two and then was dead. He also discovered that the size of the spark depended on the number of sandwiches in the pile.

After hundreds of more experiments, Volta wrote out his conclusions and sent them to the Royal Society in London. There, they were read by Sir Joseph Banks on June 26, 1800. At the time no one knew it, but this was probably the greatest event in the development of electricity! Volta had developed the first device that produced a *continual* flow of electricity.

Even so, Volta was mistaken about the source of electricity in the pile. He incorrectly assumed that electricity was produced because of the contact of different kinds of metal.°

One night after studying this controversy, Michael could not sleep. As he rolled and tossed, all he could think about were frogs and frog legs. Once as he dozed for a moment he dreamed that a huge frog was sitting at the foot of his bed. The frog was staring at him through a pair of gold-rimmed glasses. Terrified, he leaped out of bed.

Thoroughly awake, he concluded that he could have no peace of mind until he repeated Galvani's experiments. But where could he, living in the middle of London, get frog legs? The idea seemed absurd. Then suddenly he thought of a solution. Considering each angle, he knew his idea wouldn't work unless he had a yardlong piece of thread, a rubber comb, and a section of pith from the inside of a cornstalk that was as dry as a bone.

A quick glance at his table, now lighted by a full moon, showed that he already had these things. Completely satisfied, he doubled up his pillow and was soon sound asleep.

°The unit of electricty that measures pushing power is called a volt in his honor. Forty years after this, Michael Faraday showed that the electricity was produced by chemical action rather than the contact of two different metals.

6

STONE WALL

"And what is that?" asked Riebau a trifle sullenly as he stared at a marble-sized section of pulp suspended over the breakfast table by a yard of white thread.

"Michael wants to show us something," replied his wife. Her eyes slanted mischievously at Michael.

"Mmmm, some kind of magic, I suppose," snorted Riebau, his knife on a piece of bacon. "I thought you were going to be a bookbinder—"

"I am, and I like that trade very much. In addition, however, I want to be a natural philosopher."

"A natural philosopher?" Riebau reached for the pepper.

"Yes, a natural philosopher—something like Galvani and Volta. They're beginning to call them scientists."

Riebau tried to eat. But he couldn't keep his eyes from

the pulp over the table. Finally he gave up. "You must show me what this is all about," he said a little gruffly.

"You'd better show him," said Madam Riebau. "George is as curious as a cat, and if you don't show him he'll leave the table hungry!"

Michael drew a rubber comb and a wool patch from his pocket. After he had vigorously rubbed the comb on the wool a dozen or more times, he began to push the end of it toward the piece of pulp hanging over the table. From the corner of his eye he studied Riebau. His master's face was tinged with a mixture of amusement and disgust.

Then it happened! The ball of pulp was sucked through the air to the end of the comb. "The comb and the pulp are friends now," said Michael. "But just wait."

Moments later the comb all but flipped the pulp away.

"First they are married and then they are divorced," said Riebau, thoughtfully massaging his moustache. He got up and studied the pulp from several angles. Finally, he said, "Give me that comb. I'm going to try it myself."

Riebau rubbed the comb just as Michael had rubbed it. Then he pushed it toward the pulp just as Michael had done. The results were the same. "That's strange," he muttered. After a long silence, he asked, "What makes it do that?"

"I really don't know," replied Michael, speaking around a mouthful of egg. "But someday I will find out!"

"And if you find out, what good will it do?" asked Riebau, his practicality surfacing.

Michael waited until he had swallowed his food before answering. "Oh, it will do a lot of good; for it will reveal one of the hidden laws of God." He then outlined the argument between Volta and Galvani. At the end, he asked, "And do you know what happened to Professor Alessandro Giuseppe Antonio Anastasio Volta?"

"I have no idea," laughed Riebau.

"Napoleon summoned him to Paris in 1801 to demonstrate his discovery. Later, he was made a senator of the kingdom of Lombardy."

Although thoroughly impressed, Riebau commented, "He would have been better honored if they had sliced off about half his name!"

Now that the Riebaus were both laughing, Michael had a special request. With his face as serious as he could make it, he asked, "Would it be possible to h-have f-f-frog legs for s-supper?"

"Frog legs!" exploded Riebau, his eyes widening.

Michael squirmed and held his breath.

"Yes, why not?" asked his wife.

"Because—because if we're to have such a delicacy, I'd much rather have snails. Mmmm. Nothing's quite as good as snails!"

"I've already planned menus for the next three weeks," said Madam Riebau. "After that—" she closed her eyes and tapped her teeth. "Yes, after that we'll have frog legs. I'm hungry for them myself."

Michael had just started to rebind the first volume of Gibbon's *Decline and Fall of the Roman Empire* when Riebau approached with an ornamented package. "This is a special copy of *Tales from the Arabian Nights*. Deliver it to Viscount Randal in Oxford Street. Here's the address. Tomorrow is his son's birthday and he's going to give it to him for a present." Riebau was in an unusually good mood. Taking a shilling from his pocket, he added, "On the way back, buy something special for your family. Then—" He shrugged. "Then take the rest of the day off!"

As Michael hurried toward the address, he remembered the time he had read the book he was now delivering. It had held him utterly spellbound, for it was packed with altogether incredible stories. The tale of "Aladdin and the Wonderful Lamp" had especially fascinated him. Before he had started studying electricity, the magic feats of the lamp and the ring genii seemed impossible. But now, even though he knew the book was fiction, he was beginning to believe that electricity had similar possibilities. Who, for example, could adequately explain why a compass always pointed north, or how a simple Leyden jar could pack enough wallop to floor a man?

Enthused by the crisp fall day, Michael's imagination pushed out wings. Perhaps some day he could have a job in a laboratory! He might even stumble onto a new law of electricity! Indeed, electricity might eventually do for mankind what the genii did for Aladdin! Yes, in time it might be possible to send messages to a distant place in an instant—or even to produce light.

As these wild thoughts stampeded through his brain, Michael felt that he was treading in a new world of truthful magic. So excited was he that he burst out singing, "When I survey the Wondrous Cross," a popular hymn written by Dr. Isaac Watts, another dissenter with a misshapen head.°

By curious coincidence, Watts was buried at Bunhill

° His large head was out of proportion to his frail body. When the girl whom he had courted by mail saw him, she was shocked. As a result of this modest deformity he never married.

Fields, a mere few hundred yards east of the Sandemanian meetinghouse. Between the morning and evening services, Michael had often visited this cemetery and had paid special attention to the memorial stones honoring Watts, Daniel Defoe, John Bunyan, and other dissenters. The courage of these men to be different had always inspired him.

Having delivered the book, Michael started home. Just as he was leaving Oxford Street, his thoughts were interrupted by the cries of a potato vendor. "Get yourself a baked potator! Get yourself a—" sang the voice of the stoop-shouldered man.

Remembering his shilling, Michael invested in six large potatoes. "They're the finest I ever baked," boasted the man, after he had deftly raked them from his portable oven.

"Yer pa ain't been good all week," said Mrs. Faraday. "So I'm mighty glad you came. Was about to send Liz over to get you. Pa's been gatherin' some information he wants you to have."

"I've a feelin' I ain't a-gonna live long," wheezed his father from the bed. "Now I don't mind dyin'. Death is a promotion. It's like changing clothes for a weddin'. But Mike, I thought you ought to know somethin' about the family. Liz thinks yer a-gonna be famous someday, and if she's right you ought to have a speakin' knowledge of yer ancestors." After a spell of coughing, he reached for the enormous Bible on the table at his side.

Opening it with effort, he thumbed to a page where the family records were kept. "We ain't members of the nobility," he chuckled, "and so I can't take you back to William the Conqueror! Indeed, I can't take you back very far. I've heard some of my father's distant relatives came from Ireland. Don't know 'bout that. But I do know about my parents and my brothers and sisters.

"My father, Robert Faraday, married my mother, Elizabeth Dean in 1756—the year John Dean, her father, died. Grandfather Dean's will left the property to his widow. My parents, just married, managed the place.

"This forty-six acre property was known as Clapham Wood Hall, and it's near the village of Clapham in Yorkshire. Since I grew up there, I remember it well. There were lots of trees, the porch of the house and a gable end, and a little stream meandered through the place. This stream provided the power for a bobbin mill which helped provide income. Yes, Mike, it was a beautiful place and if I sound like a Yorkshireman, that's where I got my accent!

"Father had ten children, seven of 'em boys. Their birthdays are right here in the Bible. The oldest son, my brother Bob, moved to Kirkby Stephen, about 230 miles northwest of here in 1774. That was two years before Jefferson wrote the Declaration of Independence. Bob, of course, was a Sandemanian. He became a prosperous businessman and married Mary Hastwell.

"About that time, he invited me to set up a blacksmith shop at Outhgill, a tiny spot just outside Kirkby Stephen. And this I did. Then I fell in love with Margaret Hastwell, his wife's sister. In other words, brothers married sisters. This means his children are your double cousins."

"What happened to my other uncles?" asked Michael.

"Well, let's see. Richard became a grocer. John went to farming. Barnabas is a shoemaker. Tom owns a store. William died in '91. Your uncles and aunts have all done well. Some of us were a little worried about William. But he accepted Christ before he died. I have a letter from my mother that proves it—"

"You'd better rest," cautioned Mrs. Faraday from the doorway where she stood with a red apron around her waist and arms akimbo.

"Never mind, Margaret, I've got somethin' important to say to Mike—and this may be me last chance." He coughed hard. "How old are you, Mike?"

"Next week on September 22 I'll be nineteen—"

"You'll finish your apprenticeship when you're twenty-one. Robert already has his journeyman's card. This is great. Makes me feel better knowin' Margaret will have both of you to help her." Following a long interval of silence during which his mind seemed far away he motioned Michael closer. "Me and Ma are proud of the way you've taken to readin' and a-learnin' new things.

"Some at church can't understand why you read so much. Never mind them. There ain't nothin' wrong in learnin'. Remember Jesus said, 'And ye shall know the truth, and the truth shall make you free' (John 8:32).

"Most of the brothers and sisters in our church don't have no education. And yet they are good people; and the truth they know is good. Remember, Mike, truth never contradicts itself."

"Yes, Pa, I'll remember."

"One more thing. Never get so proud you can't wash your brother's feet."

"Don't worry. I won't."

As the family relaxed at the table, feasting on the potatoes and pork which Robert had provided, the conversation drifted onto electricity. "Please explain what a Leyden jar is," said Liz.

"I haven't built a Leyden jar yet," replied Michael eagerly. "But I'm going to! A month ago I noticed two bottles in a rag shop on Little Chesterfield Street. They were just what I needed. At first the owner wanted too much. I finally got them both last week for seven pence—a sixpence for the larger one and a penny for the other. The bigger bottle will be the electrostatic generator and the little one the Leyden jar. I already have—"

"Stop!" interrupted Liz, holding up her hands. "You're already over our heads. First, you must explain exactly what a Leyden jar is. I always thought Leyden was a city in Holland."

"All right, I'll explain," said Michael around a mouthful of potato. He tore some paper into bits, rubbed his comb on his pants, and demonstrated how the comb attracted the paper. "Now as far back as 1660—six years before the Great London Fire—Baron von Münchhausen built a machine to produce more electricity than is produced by rubbing amber, or even a comb.

"His machine was simply a large ball of dry sulpher which he mounted on an axle and turned rapidly. By holding his dry hands against the ball as it spun, he made a lot of sparks.

"In 1709 an Englishman, Francis Hawkesbee, improved this machine by replacing the sulpher ball with a glass globe. This worked better and wasn't so messy. Also, it didn't smell so bad. At first he produced the sparks with his dry hands. Afterwards he used pieces of rubber."°

.

°This machine and others like it simply generated the same kind of static electricity we produce when we walk across a nylon rug on a dry day.

"Michael, you'd better start eating if you don't want your food to get cold," cautioned his mother.

After swallowing one bite, Michael went on. "In 1745 E. G. von Kleist, Bishop of Pomerania, wanted to see if he could find a way to isolate electricity. And so he filled a good-sized bottle half full of water. Next, he pushed a piece of brass wire through the cork until it was submerged in the water.

"This done, he held the brass wire onto an electric machine and charged it. When he pushed the bottle away, he accidentally touched the wire and was so shocked his shoulders and arms were stunned.

"About this time, Professor van Musschenbroek in Leyden did much the same thing. Only instead of keeping still, he wrote to a distinguished friend about it. As a result such a bottle is called a Leyden jar. The new jars, of course, are not filled with water. Instead of water, they now have a metal foil on both the inside and outside."*

"And what good is a Leyden jar?" asked Elizabeth.

"Benjamin Franklin killed a turkey with one."

"But wouldn't it have been easier just to slit the turkey's throat?" she persisted.

"Of course! But that's not the point. The point is that we have discovered a vital power, and some day we will learn how to use it in a creative way. Already scientists are learning amazing things about it. A while back I was reading about Abbé Nollet. He was the first to demonstrate Leyden jars in Paris.

"One day he went to a monastery and stood the monks in a circle. He connected each monk to the next by a

---

*This same principle is used in electric condensers—a fundamental item in electronic apparatus.

piece of wire. They say the circle was more than three kilometers around. And so you can see there were a lot of monks! When everything was just right, Nollet connected the first and last monks to a series of Leyden jars. At that precise moment they were all shocked at exactly the same time. I wish I could have been there and seen them jump!"

"And what good did all of that do?" asked Elizabeth, frowning.

"It showed that maybe electricity is as fast as light. Maybe in the future it can be used to send messages. Think what would have happened if, say, one shock had stood for a and two shocks for b—and so on."

"I still think you are wasting your time with such nonsense," said Elizabeth, waving her hand.

"Do you like the baked potatoes?" asked Michael, leaning forward.

"Of course," replied Elizabeth.

"Well, when potatoes were first brought to England, many people thought they were poison," said Michael. "Indeed, some hated them so much they formed an organization to get rid of them. Their organization was called the Society for Prevention of Unwholesome Diet. The first letters of that society spell "spud," and that's our slang word for potato!"

"Oh, Michael you are impossible," said Elizabeth. "But I'm proud of you anyway!"

As Michael was completing a drawing in his notebook, he became conscious that someone was standing behind him. Turning, he faced George Riebau. "What's the matter?" he asked.

"Oh, nothing," said the Frenchman. "I was just

watching the way you write and draw. What's the purpose of all this writing and drawing?"

"Well, I know the books I love won't always be here; and so I copy those things I want to remember. It's hard work. Still, it helps me learn." He showed him some notes and drawings he had made of Benjamin Franklin's experiments.

An agonizing silence followed as Riebau held the notes to the light and leafed through them. After replacing them on the table, he slowly massaged his moustache for a long time. Then he said, "Michael, I don't want to discourage you. Nevertheless, I must speak the truth. Your drawings are terrible! Don't you know anything about perspective?"

"Perspective? What's that?"

"It's a system used by artists to show distance." He picked up the notes on Franklin. "Look at this set of wires you've drawn. They are as large on one side of the paper as they are on the other. This is incorrect."

"I g-guess I've never had anyone to teach me," said Michael, his spirits beginning to slide.

"And your writing," continued Riebau, "is not good. Don't you know that every sentence should start with a capital letter and end with a period. Have you never studied punctuation?"

"I'm afraid not. I was quite young when I quit school."

"How about sentence structure, don't you know that every sentence should have both a subject and predicate?"

"I don't even know what a subject and a p-predicate are," confessed Michael on the verge of tears.

"That's too bad," said Riebau, shaking his head. "But

75

don't worry, Michael. My wife and I are very fond of you. You are like a son, and someday you'll be an excellent bookbinder!"

After Riebau was gone, Michael thumbed through his notes. What he saw, made him sick. It was like looking through an old can of garbage. Yes, his master was right! His writing was terrible and his drawings were worse. Many sentences, although copied from an original source, were not capitalized—nor did they have the right punctuation. Suddenly a hollowness formed in his stomach and his knees felt like boiled macaroni.

By evening, the weakness in his knees, and the hollow spot in his stomach had soured into bitter despair. "I don't think I'll eat any supper," he said to Mrs. Riebau.

"We're having roast beef!" she replied.

"That sounds good," said Michael, forcing the words. "But I t-think I'd better go to bed."

Staggering over to his room, he lit a candle and slumped into bed. Alone with his thoughts, he wondered if he might not improve his English and punctuation on his own. A new grammar book had come into his possession. He had neglected it because of his interest in science. Now he opened it and began to study. Perhaps this was a solution!

But the more he studied, the more overwhelmed he became. Such difficult items as nouns, adjectives, conjunctions, prepositions, verbs, and adverbs were as incomprehensible as Egyptian hieroglyphics. Having shuddered at these horrors, he skimmed the rest of the book. There he faced such impossibilities as transitive and intransitive verbs and, even worse, dependent and independent clauses.

The discovery that such monstrosities existed gave him chills. The book reminded him of a condensed version of the London zoo. Completely frustrated, he snapped it shut and pinched out the candle.

As he tried to sleep, he felt like a chained, walled-in prisoner of ignorance under a sentence of death.

7

SWINGING DOORS

At first, science seemed easy to Michael Faraday as he read about it. All one had to do was to perform a few careful experiments and write up the results.

Fleeing the Great Plague, Sir Isaac Newton had hurried from Cambridge to his home in Woolsthorpe in 1665. While there, he noted the fall of an apple. As a direct result, he discovered the laws of gravity when he was only twenty-four.

Likewise, Galileo had discerned the first principles of motion when he was a mere twenty. He had been led to this discovery by watching the movement of a swaying lamp in the cathedral at Pisa. Later, by simultaneously dropping a one pound shot and a ten pound shot from the Leaning Tower of Pisa, he had proved that all weights—large or small—fall at the same speed.*

Others, also, had made revolutionary discoveries in a simple way. Dissenting preacher, Joseph Priestly, had discovered oxygen—he called it *dephlogisticated* air—by concentrating the sun's rays onto some red oxide of mercury through a twelve-inch magnifying glass and observing what happened.

Michael's nerves often tingled as he reread these experiments. Sometimes they became so real it seemed that he was actually sitting by the side of such greats as Newton, Volta, Priestly, Galileo, and Lavoisier. But when he tried to fathom their books he was baffled. They seemed as far over his head as the most distant stars.

Determined to understand Newton, he picked up an English translation of his best known work, *Philosophiae Naturalis Principia Mathematica.* Barely able to follow the thread of thought, Michael snapped the book shut and picked up Galileo's *Dialogues on the Two New Sciences.*

Michael knew that Galileo had gone out of his way to make this major work simple. This motive and inspired him to write in dialogue. With trusting confidence, Michael doubled up his pillow, lit an extra candle, stretched out in bed, and eagerly opened the newly bound volume. For the next several hours he and Galileo would be alone—and yet together!

Alas, he found the book was crammed with impenetrable jungles such as the following:

---

*That this experiment was performed from the Leaning Tower of Pisa has been disputed. In 1971 Dave Scott repeated Galileo's experiment on the moon by dropping a hammer and a falcon's feather at exactly the same time. Both reached the surface in precisely 1.3 seconds.

The resistance of a prism or cylinder of constant length varies in the sesquialteral ratio of its volume.

This is evident because the volume of a prism or cylinder of constant altitude varies directly as the area of its base, i.e., as the square of a side or diameter of this base; but, as just demonstrated, the resistance varies as the cube of this same side or diameter. Hence the resistance varies in the sesquialteral ratio of the volume—consequently also of the weight of the solid itself.

Again Michael snapped the book shut. This time in near anger. His eyes had sparkled when he verified Galileo's experiment by simultaneously dropping a marble and a hammer from his window. But the writings of this Italian genius were nearly as hard to understand as the incomprehensible statements of Newton!

In the dreary days that followed, Michael studied into the beginnings of those scientists who inspired him. Perhaps in their lives he would discover educational disadvantages that would encourage him. He was mistaken.

Edward Jenner, recent conqueror of smallpox, was a learned man—a doctor of medicine. Newton was a brilliant graduate of Cambridge. Galileo had been a professor at the University of Pisa. Antoine Lavoisier was a product of the Collège Nazarin. Volta and Galvani were university professors.

As Michael read about the careers of these men, his final refuge of hope seemed to close. And he was further disheartened when he considered their family backgrounds. Lavoisier's father had been a distinguished lawyer and his mother came from a wealthy family; Newton's father was "a lord of the manor" and his step-father was a well-educated rector. Galileo's father was a musician, a member of the nobility, and a successful cloth merchant.

In comparison, he, Michael Faraday, was the son of an ailing blacksmith and an illiterate mother! However, there were some encouraging facts. Many of the great men of his time were dissenters. Benjamin Franklin had had little formal training. And the current scientific rage of Europe, Humphry Davy, had served an apprenticeship just as he was serving an apprenticeship.

Michael realized that the odds against him succeeding at anything other than bookbinding were enormous.

"Michael, you look as if you've lost your last friend," said Madam Riebau at breakfast. "You haven't been eating properly—or even smiling. Cheer up. Tonight we're having frog legs for supper! Better yet, Monsieur M. Masquerier is moving in with us—"

"And why is the coming of Masquerier good news?" asked Michael as he dribbled milk on his tiny dab of porridge.

"You've been having a hard time with your drawings. This man is a famous painter. He even did a portrait of Napoleon!"

Michael lifted his eyes. "Do you think he might help me?"

"Mmmm, that depends—"

"What do you mean?"

"Since he's a refugee he'll have free time. . . . If you could get him interested in your experiments, and—and perhaps agree to do some of his room work, he might—just might—help you. We knew him in Paris years ago. He's a fine man."

All at once Michael began to feel new strength. "Will

you spare me a frog leg?" he asked eagerly.

"Of course."

After supper that evening, Michael placed the frog leg on a board and brought it into the living room. Sitting next to the guest, he said, "Monsieur Masquerier, I want to show you something."

"Ah, if I had known that there was an extra frog leg I would have had Madam cook it," said the painter with a laugh.

Michael explained the experiments of Galvani and then touched the main nerve and a muscle in the leg with sharpened iron and copper rods joined at one end. The leg twitched each time contact was made.

Masquerier's eyes twinkled. "I hope the legs I ate don't twitch in the middle of the night!" he exclaimed, pretending he was afraid.

"Don't worry about that," laughed Michael. "When those legs were in Madam's frying-pan, they twitched their last twitch."

Soon the two were bent over some of Michael's notes and drawings. "My illustrations are terrible," he confessed. "Do you think you might be able to teach me to do better?"

"Of course! Your main problem is that you don't understand perspective." He excused himself and went to his room. A few minutes later he returned with Taylor's *Perspective*. "This book will help you," he said. "And if you need any coaching, call on me."

Michael felt that God had brought Masquerier to him and that it was his duty to work hard and learn as much as possible from this colorful guest. Michael read every word in the book several times and copied all of the drawings. Several years later, George Riebau wrote a letter about these days and mailed it to a publication. With his curious system of spelling and punctuation, the French bookbinder wrote:

> . . . after the regular hours of Business, he [Michael] was chiefly employed in Drawing and Copying from the *Artists Repository* a work published in Numbers which he took in weekly—also Eliectrical Machines from the Dicty. of Arts and Sciences and other works which came in to bind. . . .
>
> If I had any curious book from my Customers to bind, with Plates, he would copy such as he thought Singular or Clever, which I advised him to Keep by him. Irelands Hogarth, and other Graphic Works, he much admired [Thomson's] Chemistry in 4 vols. he bought and interleaved a great part of it, Occasionally adding Notes with Drawings and Observations.

About this time, Michael fell in love with Mrs. Jane Marcet's *Conversations in Chemistry*. She insisted, "The most wonderful and the most interesting phenomena of nature are almost all of them produced by chemical powers." This book was extremely popular with the great number of Europeans who were following Humphry Davy's experiments and lectures in the Royal Institution on Albemarle Street.

So far, almost all of Michael's experiments had been in electricity. Now, he decided to study chemistry as well. And since he was unwilling to believe anything unless he proved it by experiment, he began to spend his few pennies in gathering apparatus.

Sometime in February, 1810, Michael learned about a series of lectures that were being given by John Tatum every other Wednesday in his home at 53 Dorset Street. Since the lectures started at 8:00 p.m., Michael was free to attend. But there was a problem. Money! Each lecture cost one shilling.

Fortunately Michael's brother Robert heard about this problem and gave him the money to attend twelve of the lectures. Since Michael felt that this was his great opportunity, he resolved to receive—and retain—the maximum benefit.

With collar high for protection against the February chill, Michael stepped into the street and headed toward the home of John Tatum. A nervous check indicated that he had an abundance of writing material. Assured, he lowered his head and pushed through the wind.

Michael had learned that Tatum was the guiding spirit of the City Philosophical Society—a group of young men that had been organized in 1808. This society sponsored the lectures.

Arriving a few minutes early, Michael was introduced to several members, including Edward Magrath and Richard Phillips—editor of the *Philosophical Magazine*. As he listened to various conversations, it became apparent that everyone present was years ahead of him educationally. Even some of the words and ideas in their idle chatter were over his head.

Michael felt grim, out of place. But after a short inward struggle, he determined to follow a relentless course. He would work harder than any of them! He would burn three candles to their one. When Tatum began to speak, Michael was ready.

During this series of lectures, Michael developed a system to record them. From his own words we can see how this was done.

My method was to take with me a sheet or two of paper

stitched or pinned up to the middle so as to form something like a book. I usually got a front seat and there placed my hat on my knees and paper on the hat. . . . [As] Mr. Tatum proceeded on in his lecture [I] set down the most prominent words, short but important sentences, titles of the experiments, names of what subjects came under consideration, and many other hints that would tend to bring what had passed into my mind. . . .

On leaving the lecture room I proceeded immediately homeward and in that and the next night had generally drawn up a second set of notes from the first. . . .

These second set of notes were my guide whilst writing out the lecture in a rough manner. They gave me the order in which the different parts came under consideration and in which the experiments were performed and they called to mind the most important subjects that were discussed. I then referred to memory for the matter belonging to each subject and I believe that I have not let much of the meaning and sense of Mr. Tatum's lectures slip. . . .

As I ultimately referred to memory for the whole of the lecture it is not to be supposed that I could write it out in Mr. Tatum's own words. I was obliged to compose it myself.

With Michael's system, he was exposed to each lecture at least four times! (1) When he heard it. (2) When he wrote it out in abbreviated notes. (3) When he enlarged the notes. And (4) when he wrote the entire lecture in his own words.

In addition to this, he made careful illustrations of the experiments; and if he had the apparatus, he repeated the experiments. At this point, Riebau agreed that he could use a part of the bindery for a laboratory.

The fireplace that warmed the room became a furnace at night, and the mantlepiece that supported books during the day, held tubes and bottles at night.

As the lectures continued, Michael's thirst for

knowledge increased. Sometimes the lecture was on something he knew nothing about and in which he had no concern. Nevertheless, he made a full record and, if possible, performed verifying experiments.

Toward the end of the series, Michael had learned so much he occasionally disagreed with the lecturer! In the lecture titled "Mechanics," Michael noted:

> I am now going to enter upon a description of the mechanic power: but I think it necessary to remark that I have here proceeded in a different order to that which Mr. Tatum pursued when speaking of them. He first explained the pulley then the wheel and axle, and lastly the lever; but as both the pulley and the wheel are much easier explained when considered as levers, I thought it proper to enter upon the consideration of a simple lever before we proceeded to the more compound states of it.

Michael's understanding of science grew rapidly. Still, he was anxious about his English. After a lecture, he explained his problem to John Tatum.

"Why don't you ask Edward Magrath to help you?" asked Tatum.

"D-do you think he would?"

"I've always found him generous. . . . Perhaps you could exchange knowledge. Since your brain is like a sponge, you have a lot to offer."

Magrath agreed and set up a weekly two-hour study with Michael. This mutual sharing of knowledge went on for seven years! As the two continued to meet, others joined them. The agreement of the group, which had expanded to half a dozen, was to be extremely frank, to work hard, and never to leave in anger—regardless of the comments!

A new reprint of Isaac Watts' book, *The Improvement of the Mind*, mysteriously came to Michael's attention. Glancing through it while waiting for the glue on the spine of a book to dry, he found that it was slanted toward young people. Its purpose was exactly what he needed: self-improvement.

Having sung Watts' hymns and having visited his grave many times, Michael was already a devoted follower. Being a dissenter, and coming from a family of dissenters, Watts, like Michael, had had a hard time. As an infant, he had been nursed by his mother while she visited his father in a foul prison where he languished because of his faith.

That evening Michael settled into bed with Watts' book in his hand. Perhaps this book—it had taken Watts twenty years to write—would be the key to open the door to his life's work! Soon the wings of his imagination were flapping as he read:

> A well-furnished library and a capacious memory are indeed of singular use toward the improvement of the mind; but if all of your learning be nothing else but a mere amassment of what others have written, without a due penetration of their meaning, and without a judicious and determination of your own sentiments, I do not see what title your head has to true learning above your shelves . . . with the neglect of your reasoning powers, you can justly claim no higher character but that of a good historian of the sciences.

As Michael read this, he was in total agreement. Many of his friends in the City Philosophical Society were merely historians! A ferment deep inside Michael kept him from being a parrot. This ferment had lured him to Galileo. Galileo's world had been dominated by Aristotle, even though that ancient Greek had been dead for around 2,000 years! In his day, a quotation from Aristotle followed by the words *magister dixit*—the master has spoken—settled all arguments.

In spite of this, Galileo had had the courage to flagrantly defy Aristotle even though the Inquistion foamed and snarled and threatened to burn him at the stake. And because of Galileo, many new laws—God's laws—had been discovered. These laws had made the world a much better place in which to live.

Already Michael knew that his views of electricity were in conflict with those of John Tatum. Whereas Tatum believed in Franklin's "one-fluid" theory, Michael believed in the "two-fluid" theory as advanced by Tytler and others. Moreover, he had agreed to give a lecture—his first—to the Society on his views!

As he studied the book, Michael found that he was already doing a number of things advocated by Watts. He was attending lectures, keeping notes, and meeting in weekly sessions with friends. There was one major thing, however, which he was not doing. Watts emphasized that it would be beneficial to carry on a long correspondence with an equal or superior person who was in a position to help. With this in mind, Michael began to look for such a person.

Providentually, he didn't have long to wait. Tatum introduced Michael to Benjamin Abbott, a young man about his own age. Abbott was a devout Quaker and had an excellent education. He earned his living as a confidential secretary in the city. Also, he was interested in chemistry. Soon they were meeting in Abbott's father's house in Long Lane. In the midst of an experiment, Michael had an idea. "Let's discuss our problems and experiments by mail. That way we will have permanent records to review," he suggested.

Abbott agreed and so a long and valued correspondence began which was to continue for many years.

In 1809 the Faradays moved to 18 Weymouth Street. This was a few blocks northeast of their old home in Jacob's Well Mews and thus a little closer to their meetinghouse. The new home had two extra rooms that could house boarders in case of financial emergency. James Faraday continued to fail. In a letter to a brother, he wrote: "I never expect to be clear of the pain completely with which I am afflicted, yet I am glad to say that I am somewhat better."

Improvement didn't last. He died at Weymouth Street on October 30, 1810. In keeping with Sandemanian custom, the funeral was conducted in utter silence. As Michael watched the cheap casket slowly sinking into the deep wound in the earth, memory flung him back to the day his father had given him the family genealogy.

While gripping his hand, James Faraday had reminded him of the words of Jesus: "And ye shall know the truth, and the truth shall make you free." Suddenly Michael's eyes were moist. Yes, he believed those words were true. Indeed, they had become a part of himself!

8

FOUR TICKETS

"Monsieur Riebau tells me you're interested in science," said Mr. Dance, speaking across the counter at No. 2 Blandford Street.

"I certainly am, and have been for a long time," replied Michael. "And in a way, you're responsible!"

"How's that?"

"Remember when you looked up some words for me in Johnson's *Dictionary*—and then showed me your *Britannica?*"

"Of course. But how did that interest you in science?"

"It interested me in looking up things. About that time someone brought in a set of *Britannica*. . . . By chance I read James Tytler's article on electricity. That article lit a fuse! Soon I read every article in *Britannica* on the subject. Now I'm hooked."

"Very interesting, Mr. Faraday. Very interesting," said Dance, beaming. "Perhaps you know that I'm a member of the Royal Institution. This means that science is a part of my life." He thoughtfully bit his lip and withdrew some tickets from his waistcoat pocket. "How would you like to hear a lecture by Humphry Davy?"

"You mean the Davy who just discovered the new elements—barium, boron, calcium, and—let's see—potassium!" exclaimed Michael, his heart thumping.

"Who else? There's only one Humphry Davy!"

"I would give my right arm to hear one. But it's impossible. You see, Mr. Dance, I'm only an apprentice—"

"Nonsense. I have these four tickets, and they're yours—free."

The tickets were dated February 29, March 14, April 8, and April 10, 1812. As Michael stared at these oblong pieces of cardboard he was so overwhelmed he was speechless. To him, they were like passes to paradise. Dance saved him from embarrassment by tipping his hat and stepping into the street.

Work finished, Michael all but ran home.

"Guess what?" he exclaimed.

"You're going to bind a book for the Prince of Wales?" ventured Liz.

"No, it's better than that!"

"You found fifty pounds in an old book," suggested his mother.

"No, no. It's better than that. Much better—"

"Well, tell us," said Liz. She lifted an iron from the stove and tested its heat with a spot of saliva.

"I'm going to hear four lectures at the Royal Institution by no other than Humphry Davy—the greatest scientist in the world!"

"I wish I could go with you," sighed Elizabeth. "I know a girl who heard him. She said that he was the greatest speaker that she had ever heard, and that he has beautiful eyes—"

As Michael awaited the date of the first lecture, he reread Mrs. Marcet's *Conversations in Chemistry*. He realized that many of her stories about Davy were dated. This was because Davy seemed to come up with a sensationally new discovery every other week. Nevertheless, he went over every word and drawing in his now nearly wornout copy. He was determined to have the best possible background for anything that might be said.

Thoughts of the coming lectures charged Michael as if he were a Leyden jar, and when he lingered with his daydreams it seemed that exploding sparks of electricity bumped down his spine.

On February 29—it was leap year—Michael arrived at the Royal Institution on Albemarle Street nearly an hour early. As only a few were present, he walked around the horseshoe-shaped auditorium. Since the floor slanted downward toward the platform, he decided to sit in the balcony right over the clock. This position would give him a better view than any place in the building. While he waited, an usher handed him a pamphlet.

"It will tell you something about the Royal Institution," he said.

The Institution, Michael learned, had been founded in 1799 by a Massachusetts Yankee—Benjamin Thompson. During the American Revolution, Thompson's Royalist sympathies had driven him from the Colonies. A grateful King George III had knighted him; and later, in Bavaria, he was made a count of the Holy Roman Empire. Upon his return to England, he chose to be known as Count Rumford.

The purpose of the Institution was to encourage scientific study, and it had been doing exactly that ever since King George had granted it a charter in 1800.

Soon the place exploded into life with crowds of the best dressed people Michael had ever seen. "Mind if I sit next to you?" chimed a voice.

"Oh, it's you, Mr. Dance!" exclaimed Michael, leaping to his feet and extending his hand. "It's impossible for you to know how grateful I am for this privilege." A quarter of an hour later their conversation was interrupted by thunderous cheers from the eager listeners who packed every seat.

Humphry Davy had entered and was slowly walking toward his place in the U of the large table loaded with apparatus. Glowing with a wide smile, he waited until the applause subsided. Then in a slow, dramatic way, he began, "Ladies and gentlemen—"

Michael knew that in addition to his scientific ability Davy was a talented author. Even the celebrated Coleridge praised his poetry. Now, as he listened to the speaker's fine voice and nearly perfect diction, he was convinced that the author of *The Rime of the Ancient Mariner* was correct.

All at once Davy began to talk about potassium—a new element he had discovered and named. Edging forward, Michael began to write furiously and make illustrations. This was one of the discoveries that had flung the name of Humphry Davy around the world! Michael had pored over the details of that discovery many times.

In the fall of 1807, Davy felt that he might decompose

"saturated solutions of potash and soda" by sending an electrical current through them. Assembling all of the batteries in the Royal Institution—nearly three hundred plates of copper and zinc—he connected them in series and made the attempt. All he produced was oxygen and hydrogen and that "with much heat and effervescence."

Next, he tried heating the potash alone "by means of a stream of oxygen gas ... which was thrown on a [platinum] spoon containing potash." When the potash was "in a state of perfect fluidity" he applied current. This produced potassium.

Davy's cousin, Edmund Davy, who worked as his assistant at the time, recorded Humphry's jubilation. "When he saw the minute globules of potassium burst through the crust of potash, and take fire as they entered the atmosphere, he could not contain his joy—he actually danced about the room in ecstatic delight. . . ."

After relating how he had isolated potassium on that sixth day of October, Davy said, "Now I will show you how it is done." As he spoke, his assistant—later Michael learned his name was William Payne—produced the apparatus just as it was needed. Davy now heated potash until it turned liquid. Then he switched on the current from a 250-plate battery.

As the nearly breathless audience strained to watch, shiny blue and white beads began to assemble. Gathering bits of them, Davy said, "This silver white metallic element is potassium. In time we will undoubtedly find many uses for it.° Please watch as I toss it into this basin of water."

For a moment the gleaming metal floated. Then the

° It is now used in fertilizer, medicine, dyeing, and photography.

water began to burn with a bright, purple flame. It was pure magic—fully equal to that produced by Aladdin's genii! Once again the crowd was on its feet, cheering and clapping.

Michael was utterly spellbound.

At another lecture, Davy illuminated the entire auditorium by forming an arc between two pieces of carbon connected to a 1,000-plate battery. For a brief moment the place was lighter than day.

Walking home with Mr. Dance after the last lecture, Michael said, "If I could manage it, I would give up bookbinding for science."

"Nonsense!" replied Dance, moving to the right to avoid a hole in the street. "There isn't much money in science, and it would be extremely hard to get a position. Besides, aren't you about ready to finish your apprenticeship?"

"I'll be through on October 12."

The two continued on together in silence for a full city block. Then Michael stopped. "I almost envy that assistant," he said. "Do you, sir, think there might be a chance for me to get a job in the Royal Institution, perhaps as an assistant? I'd be glad to do anything!"

"I really don't know," replied Mr. Dance. "But if I ever hear of an opening, I'll let you know."

Michael tried desperately to get to sleep. It was impossible. All he could think about was what he had learned at the lectures. He knew that Davy had changed assistants before. Could it be that he might do so again? Suddenly an idea possessed him.

Lighting a candle, he selected a sheet of paper and boldly addressed a letter to Sir Joseph Banks, President of the Royal Institution. Straining to use the best spelling he knew, Michael explained his interest in science and applied for a job.

Hours after mailing the application, he marveled at his courage. Everyone knew that Sir Joseph was an important scientist. His credentials were most impressive. After attending Harrow and Eton, he had spent three years at Oxford. Later, he made a three-year voyage with none other than Captain James Cook—discoverer of Hawaii!

Banks had been knighted, made a Commander of the Bath, and was elected President of the Royal Institution in 1788. In addition, he was wealthy, and was recognized as one of the world's great botanists.

For a moment, had it been possible, Michael would have snatched his letter from the mails. Since this couldn't be done, he waited—and prayed!

Day after day he labored on the notes of Davy's lectures. When he was finished, the notes made a good-sized book. Next, he titled the book and bound it in leather. On April 8, two days before his last lecture, Davy was knighted by the Prince Regent.° Three days later he married Mrs. Apreece, a rich Scottish widow and a relative of Sir Walter Scott. These events intrigued Michael.

They made him treasure his beautifully bound notes even more.

As Michael awaited an answer to his application, the minutes and even the seconds seemed to lengthen. He watched the mails like a sleuth from Scotland Yard. Finally, at the end of two weeks, his patience was so

---

° He followed his father George III to the throne after his father had gone hopelessly insane in 1811. Later, he was coronated as George IV. This was the first knighthood he conferred on anyone.

exhausted he decided on a daring move. He decided to call on Sir Joseph Banks personally—at his home!

As Michael stepped through the ornate arch and walked past the magnificent formations of dazzling flowers which Sir Joseph had gathered from worldwide trips, he could feel his heart squirming beneath his coat. It seemed foolhardy that he, a not-yet-finished apprentice, would make such a call. With effort, he forced his feet up the path and pulled the elaborate door knocker.

"May I 'elp you?" demanded the porter, a tall cockney imprisoned in stiff uniform.

With a vain attempt to keep the quiver out of his voice, Michael explained the purpose of his call.

"Remain 'ere and I'll check," said the man.

Minutes later, the doorman returned with the application. Scrawled across the front, were the words: "No answer." Struggling with emotion, Michael jammed the letter in his pocket and returned to the bindery. It seemed that his world was tearing apart, and these feelings were accentuated by the happenings of the time.

That spring with 600,000 men under his command, Napoleon headed toward Moscow determined to smash Russia, and on June 18 the United States declared war on Britain.° Michael read the headlines about these events and yet he had a minimum of concern. His brain had only one focus: science!

With the end of his apprenticeship a mere three months away, Michael became increasingly anxious

---

°Although hard to believe, the facts indicate that the four tickets given to Michael Faraday ultimately had more effect on changing the world than either of these events. This is so even though a mere 30, 000 of Napoleon's men survived the Russian winter.

about the future. Robert had now married. This meant that Michael needed to provide even more of the support for his mother and sisters. He prayed for guidance.

Shoving disappointment from his mind, he burned his extra energy by studying his notes and performing experiments. On July 12 he mailed his first letter to Benjamin Abbott. His grammar and spelling were still extremely bad. Still, he felt that writing to a friend was the best way to improve. Included in this many-page document is his description of a project.

I have lately made a few simple galvanic experiments merely to illustrate to myself the first principles of science. I was going to Knights, to obtain some nickle & bethought me, that they had Malleable Zinc: I enquired & boght some.—have you seen any yet? The first portion I obtained was in the thinnest pieces possible; observe in a flattened state. It was as they informed me, thin enough for the Electric Snake, or as I before called it, de Luc's Electric column.° I obtained it for the purpose of forming discs, with which & copper to make a little battery. the first I completed contained the immense number of seven Plates!!! and of the immense size of half-pence each!!!!

He then explained how he had used this material.

I, Sir, I my own self, cut out seven discs of the size of half-pennies each! I, Sir, covered them with seven half-pence and I interposed between seven or rather six pieces of paper, soaked in muriate of Soda!!!—but laugh no longer Dear A_____ rather wonder at the effects this trivial power produced, it was sufficient to produce the decomposition of the Sulphate of Magnesia; an effect which extremely surprised me, for I did not—could not have any Idea that the agent was competent to the purpose.—"

° He was probably referring to a voltaic pile.

After long further description of this self-built voltaic pile, he added an observation:

> Another Phenomena I observed was this, on separating the discs from each other, I found that some of the zinc discs had got a coating, a very superficial one. . . . I think this circumstance well worth notice, for remember no effect takes place without a cause. . . .*

He signed the letter:

> I am dear A____
> Yours Sincerely
> M. Faraday

Michael's apprenticeship had been pleasant. Monsieur Riebau was so satisfied with his work he had given him the oversight of two other apprentices. (One of these became a comedian and the other a professional singer!) As his final day, October 12, approached, Michael's heaviness of heart increased.

Monsieur and Madam Riebau had been extremely good to him!

After kissing him affectionately on both cheeks, Riebau said, "Michael, De la Roche, your new master, is a good man. Sometimes he growls like a hungry lion in the zoo, but he never bites—at least not hard!"

"Be sure and come back and see us," added Madam Riebau, dabbing at her eyes with the corner of her apron. "Remember that we consider you to be almost the same as a son."

"I won't be able to stay away," replied Michael, struggling unsuccessfully with tears.

---

*This phenomenon is the basis for electroplating.

9

UNEMPLOYED

Like Riebau, Monsieur De la Roche was a French refugee. Inclined to be stout, he sported a trim moustache. It was cropped close to the skin and spread across his lip like a black ribbon.

During the first week, Michael felt Riebau's comparison of De la Roche to a growling lion to be grossly exaggerated. Then it happened. A man came in to examine a new edition of Sam Johnson's *Dictionary*. After viewing the expensive binding and discussing the price, he left without buying it.

"You should have made that sale!" snarled De la Roche.

"He said he wanted to think about it."

"Think about it? Bah! He doesn't need to think about it! He has more money than he can spend in seven lifetimes. Michael Faraday, you are an abominable salesman!"

"I'm not a salesman, sir, I'm a bookbinder."

"If you're going to work here, you've got to do some selling. Business is terrible. I can't afford another clerk. I—"

The tirade was interrupted by the appearance of a customer.

Next day, De la Roche sold a new set of *Britannica*. The sale changed him into a new man. "Michael," he purred, "you are the best bookbinder I've ever met! I doubt if your equal could be found in all of London—or even Paris. That last Bible you bound is perfect!"

The purring didn't last. Within three days De la Roche was so angry he picked up a pot of glue and Michael ducked, fearing he might hurl it at him.

Completely shaken, Michael approached his mother. Speaking across the supper table, he said, "He acts like a demon. I can't stand it much longer. Besides, my heart is in science; not bookbinding."

"Then get a job in science."

"But even if I got one, the pay wouldn't be much."

"That don't make no difference. God will supply. He has in the past and He will in the future. Remember the sparrows—"

"Oh, Ma, you make me so proud," said Michael, pacing about. "There aren't many mothers as courageous as you!"

Two weeks later Michael told De la Roche he was quitting.

"But you can't do that!" exploded the Frenchman.

"I've made up my mind. I'm already twenty-one and

if I'm to be a scientist I had better start now."

"Do you have a job?"

"Not yet."

Suddenly De la Roche was sniffling. "If you'll promise to stay with me the rest of my life, I'll make you my sole heir. What do you think of that Mr. Faraday?"

"I-I think it's a most generous offer, Monsieur. Nevertheless, I'm afraid I cannot accept. I'm going to be a scientist even if I freeze or have nothing to eat!"

As a chilly November and early December stabbed frozen fingers through the streets of London, Michael paced the city looking for work. He scoured business areas, visited establishments along Oxford and Fleet Streets, and wandered up and down Crooked Lane and Scalding Alley.

There were no openings and the managers assured him that there were not about to be any openings. "Now that Puss and Boots has lost his army in Russia, England is re-laxing. Soon a lot of soldiers will be looking for work. Grim days lie ahead," explained the owner of a medical supply house.

While shuffling down Milk Street after a weary day of refusals, Michael was stopped by an old woman pushing a cart. "You ain't a-lookin' fer work are ye?" she asked. peering at him out of her one good eye. " 'Ow'd ya like to make some big money, say a pound a day?"

"I'd like that very much. Any ideas?"

She motioned him into an alley. "Now there ain't no reason fer you nor your ma to be 'ungry. I need some 'elp badly and I believe yer jist wot I needs."

"Doing what?" asked Michael. Her dirty nails and black stumps of teeth had made him wary.

"Diggin' up bodies. I'm a resurrection woman."

"A resurrection woman! What's that?"

"Oh, we dig up bodies and sell 'em to the doctors—"

"Human bodies?"

"Of course! The doctors need 'em to study their insides. "Ow will they learn about livers and sich if they don't cut up a few bodies? Now it ain't as bad as it sounds. You see we dig up the bodies at night. That way the weepin' relatives don't know nothin' 'bout it. Of course sometimes we git the bodies fer free and without no trouble like when the poor die in the streets or the criminals git their necks stretched at Tyburn."

"I'd starve before I'd do that!" shuddered Michael, walking away.

Robert was all aglow as he visited at Weymouth Street. Facing Michael across the living room, he asked, "How'd you like to make eight hundred pounds a year?"

"I can't even imagine that much money," said Michael.

"Since I switched to the gas works I've done real well. Soon, all of London will be lit by gas. There will be miles and miles of it. Spoke to my boss about you. He's definitely interested. . . ."

Michael called the next day.

"Do you know anything about mathematics and mensuration?" asked the fierce-looking employer.

"I'm afraid not, sir," stammered Michael. "My training is in chemistry and electricity—especially electricity."

"Electricity is a waste of time. It's just a toy. Gas is the thing! Soon every building in London will be lit by gas."

Michael expressed his disappointment in a letter to Abbott.

Dear A ———

I am just now involved in a fit of vexation. I have an excellent prospect before me and cannot take it up. . . . Alas Alas Inability——I must ask your advice and intend if I can see you. . . .

"Michael, you look as if you've lost your last friend," said Monsieur Masquerier. "What's the matter?"

"I'm out of work, and I have to support my mother and sisters."

"Maybe you shouldn't have given up bookbinding. De la Roche was brokenhearted when you left. He actually wept. Tell me, if you had to do it over again would you still quit?"

"Of course! I'm going to be a scientist. I want to learn God's laws, sooner or later the door will open. And yet in the meantime I get discouraged. I—"

"How about taking a walk with me?" asked the painter, reaching for his hat. "Nothing inspires me more than a walk. . . ."

As they headed south toward the Houses of Parliament, Masquerier was in an unusually thoughtful mood. "Mr. Faraday, I've always admired you—especially for your determination and religious faith. Some day you'll make your mark. It takes courage to swim upstream, especially when hunters stand on the banks and shoot at you. But you have the courage to swim upstream, there's no doubt about that."

"The great things in the world are done by people with determination. Take Rembrandt for example. He all but starved. To him, however, that didn't matter. He determined that he would paint masterpieces, and he did just that."

Soon they were walking along the banks of the

Thames. "On my first visit to London there were slave ships here," said Masquerier. "Now, there are none. Why?"

"I don't know."

"There aren't any more slavers because the British slave trade was abolished in 1807. And it was abolished because of William Wilberforce, a little, half-blind man who would not give up. Several times I heard him speak in the House of Commons. He was dominated by the belief that slavery is wrong."°

The pair entered the House of Commons and briefly listened to a snatch of a debate on the current war with the United States. Next, they sauntered over to Westminster Abbey.

"I love to come here," whispered Masquerier. "The quiet and the arches and the statues inspire me." He led Michael to the tomb of Sir Isaac Newton. With heads uncovered, they stood in awe as they read the inscription which concluded:

Let Mortals rejoice
That there has existed such and so great
An ornament of the human race.

On their way back to Blandford Street, Michael remarked, "One of the things I like about Newton is that he was a God-fearing man. Indeed, in all his studies he felt that he was merely following the footsteps of the Eternal!"

After two blocks of silence, Masquerier stopped. Gripping the lapels of Michael's coat with both hands, he

---

°For an interesting book on Wilberforce see *He Freed Britain's Slaves*, by Charles Ludwig, Herald Press, 1977.

said, "I just thought of something that is most remarkable. Michaelangelo died in 1564. That was the year Galileo was born. In turn, Galileo died in 1642; and that was the year Sir Isaac Newton was born." He closed his eyes and massaged his chin.

"And what year were you born, Mr. Faraday?"

"1791."

"That is most remarkable. You were born just three years before our own Antoine Lavoisier was guillotined in the Reign of Terror."

"And what does that mean?" asked Michael.

"What does it mean? It means that maybe you are destined to carry on the work of this man who taught us that we can neither create nor destroy and that all fires burn oxygen!"

"I appreciate your confidence, sir. But your dreams are impossible. I have no formal education. I have no knowledge of mathematics. I can't even punctuate or spell."

"Nonsense! You can read, and that is all that is necessary! At the pinnacle of his fame, Newton said, 'If I have seen farther, it is by standing on the shoulders of giants.' Mr. Faraday, that is what you must do. You must stand on the shoulders of giants!"

Following an excellent meal with the Riebaus, Michael's former master said, "Michael, why don't you send a letter of application to Sir Humphry Davy, and along with the letter enclose that beautifully bound notebook you made of his lectures? That notebook just might open the door."

"I think he's right," agreed Masquerier. "And if I were you, I would do it right away!"

After selecting the finest paper he possessed, Michael carefully addressed a letter to Sir Humphry in which he explained his interest in science. He rewrote the letter three times before he was satisfied. The next evening he handed the letter together with the notebook to the porter at the Royal Institution.

Feeling that long days of waiting were ahead, Michael went back to his experiments and correspondence. In a letter to Abbott dated December 7, he praised him for the lecture he had given at Tatum's and apologized for not answering any of his last six letters. That he was discouraged is indicated in a line near the bottom of the page: "I must resign my occupation till a future time."

As the short days and long nights crept slowly by, Michael's anxiety increased. Each time he returned home, his first question was, "Any mail for me?" On seven occasions he waded through deep snow to the post office to double-check. There was none.

Soon the Christmas season arrived. Store windows filled with wreathes, bakeries displayed mince pies— some of them a yard across, carolers with scarfs at their throats thronged the streets, restaurants overflowed, and flower girls shivered on the corners hoping to sell a few flowers.

Sandemanians respected Christmas, but they did not celebrate it as elaborately as did the Anglicans and Roman Catholics.

"I don't think Sir Humphry will ever answer your letter. Sir Joseph Banks didn't. You're just wasting your time being so anxious," said Elizabeth.

"Oh, yes he will," assured Mrs. Faraday. "Where's your faith?"

"We'll see," replied Elizabeth confidentally.

That Christmas Eve there was a sudden pounding on the door.

"See who it is," said Mrs. Faraday, a platter in her hand.

Glancing out the window through the frost, Michael saw a smart carriage near the door. Opening it, he faced a messenger in trim uniform. "Letter for Mr. Michael Faraday," barked the man.

"I'm Michael Faraday," said Michael, reaching for it.

As the messenger retired to his carriage, Michael broke the wax seal and unfolded the letter.

"Brrrr. Close the door!" shouted Elizabeth.

After kicking the door shut with his heel, Michael read the letter in one glance. Then, in a tone of ecstasy, he read it out loud.

Mr. M. Faraday, 188, Weymouth Street, Portland Place.

December 24, 1812.

Sir,—I am far from displeased with the proof you have given me of your confidence, and which displays great zeal, power of memory, and attention. I am obliged to go out of town, and shall not be settled in town till the end of January; I will then see you any time you wish. It would gratify me to be of any service to you. I wish it may be in my power.

I am Sir
your obt. humble servt.
H. Davy.

After reading the letter at least twenty times, Michael sank into a chair. He was utterly exhausted. But a moment later he was on his feet again. "Just think," he exulted. "This is Christmas Eve and Sir Isaac Newton was born on Christmas Day. Moreover, I was born on

September 22 while Antoine Lavoisier was born on August 26 and I was less than three when he was guillotined!"

"And what does all of that mean?" demanded Elizabeth.

"What does that mean?" exclaimed Michael. "It means a lot. But you'd never understand because you're not a scientist!"

10

ASSISTANT TO SIR
HUMPHRY

According to his letter, Davy would not return to London until the end of January. This meant a minimum of five weeks before he could be interviewed. An endless length of time, it seemed.

Michael determined to spend every minute in preparing for the event. When he asked Robert if he could borrow his suit for the occasion, his brother agreed provided "he didn't spill acid on it."

Sir Humphry's latest book, *Elements of Chemical Philosophy*, published that spring, was causing a stir in scientific circles. Michael had read it in the nearby British Museum. Now he decided to borrow a copy from Abbott or John Tatum. Also, he planned to perform all of the experiments for which he had the necessary apparatus. He smiled as he contemplated this work. He firmly agreed that Sir Humphry was correct in declaring chlorine to be an element!

The date for the interview was set for early February. Michael dressed as carefully as possible. "I don't want to be overdressed," he nervously remarked to Liz as she gave him final inspection.

After critically viewing his velvet breeches, stockings, and formal, swallow-tail coat, she said, "You look just perfectly right. I shall be prayin' fer you."

Michael and Sir Humphry met in an upstairs room in the Royal Institution in front of a high, well-draped window.° Michael was astonished at what he saw. Davy was carelessly dressed. There were acid holes in his coat. His fingers were stained.

Both were slender and about five feet seven inches in height. But whereas Faraday parted his hair in the middle, Sir Humphry combed his slightly forward.

"I loved your notes, Mr. Faraday," said Sir Humphry, still standing. "You have an excellent hand and your drawings are great. Now what can I do for you?"

"Please, Sir Humphry, I-I'd like to work here. You see, I-I want to be a scientist!"

"Mmmm. Scientists don't make much money. You're an excellent bookbinder. . . ." Peering at him closely in the same manner in which he examined a chemical phenomenon, he demanded, "Why would you want to change professions?"

"Because—because all I can think about is science."

"How much formal education do you have?"

° Because of the progress that resulted from this interview, Sir William Bragg, director of the Royal Institution in 1935 sent out a Christmas greeting featuring this scene.

"Very little. I only attended school for a year. But I've been to many of John Tatum's lectures and I've given a lecture or two myself. Also I've done a lot of reading and a friend has been tutoring me two hours a week. I just read *Elements of Chemical Philosophy*. It's an excellent book, sir. I especially like the introduction in which you gave the history of chemistry."

Davy frowned. "I think you're overly concerned about a lack of formal education. I have only a smattering more than you. The thing that really counts is how much one is willing to work."

"Sir Humphry, I quite agree with you that chlorine is an element," wedged in Michael hurriedly. He feared he was losing Davy's interest.

"I'm glad to know that and I wish I could offer you a position. However, none is available. If I were you, I'd return to bookbinding. Now if you'll excuse me, I have stacks of work to do. I'm preparing an article for the *Quarterly Journal of Science*.

An inward numbness gripped Michael even before he stepped into the raw weather. It seemed every door was nailed, barricaded, and bolted. Still, he had tried. Also, he had shaken hands and conversed with the great Sir Humphry Davy! Already he could envision the astonishment that would appear in Abbott's eyes when he related the story.

"Don't worry, Michael," comforted his mother. "God has big plans for you. I feel it in me bones."

The next week there was another thump at the door.

"Sir Humphry wants me to work for him for three days!" exclaimed Michael after he had devoured the letter. "At last I'll have my chance!"

"I'm crushed with work," announced Davy, a tube in one hand and a flask in the other. "I want you to copy these notes so that I can send them to the editor. Use the room down the hall."

Michael's task was not easy. He found that Davy's spelling was nearly as bad as his own, and that his handwriting was a museum of horrors. Had it not been that Michael knew approximately what Davy had intended to say, he would have been forced to give up. Also, Sir Humphry often crossed out mistakes by smearing them over with his finger after he had dipped it in ink. This reduced numerous pages to a near-swamp of smudges and fingerprints. By evening, Michael was exhausted.

At the end of the third day, the assignment completed, Michael was paid and told that there was no more work. "It was nice to have met you," said Sir Humphry at the door. Again Michael's insides felt like ice in the Thames.

By the end of the month, however, the carriage once again halted at the Faraday home. This time the letter assured him that he was needed as an assistant.

"Your job," said Sir Humphry, "will be to keep the floors swept, the inkwells filled, and all the apparatus cleaned. You will also help with the lectures. The pay is a guinea a week plus room, together with heat and candles. Also we supply aprons. What is your answer?"

"I accept!" said Michael.

So it was that Michael started his career at the Royal Institution on March 1, 1813.° He was given the job be-

---

°The minutes of the Royal Institution read: "Resolved—That Michael Faraday be engaged to fill the situation lately occupied by Mr. Payne on the same terms."

cause William Payne, the former assistant, was involved in a brawl. He had attacked the instrument maker.

Following tedius days of floor scrubbing, Michael was excited when Sir Humphry approached with a request. "Here are some sugar beets. Extract the sugar; and when you're through with that, make some carbon disulfide."

"Yes, Sir Humphry," replied Michael eagerly. These were routine tasks and he soon completed them satisfactorily. It seemed that he was as close to paradise as it is possible for a human to be while still on earth. At the Institute he had complete access to a vast scientific library, an excellent laboratory, and a superb collection of scientific journals which were kept up to date.

Within six weeks of his employment, Michael's pen was skimming across paper as he kept his friends informed on his activities. His excitement can be discerned between the lines even though they are carelessly written and filled with bad grammar. This one was to Abbott:

Agreeable to what I have said above I shall at this time proceed to acquaint you with the results of some more experiments on the detonating·compound of Chlorine and Azote. . . . I am happy to say I do it at my ease for I have escaped (not quite unhurt) from four different and strong explosions of the substance. . . . It exploded by the slight heat of a small piece of cement that touched the glass above half an inch from the substance. . . . The expansion was so rapid as to blow my hand open, tear off a part of one nail and has made my finger so sore that I cannot yet use them easily— The pieces of tube were projected with such force as to cut the glass face of the mask I had on. . . ."

Although extremely busy with his laboratory work, Michael continued his weekly studies with Magrath.

Toward the end of September, Sir Humphry invited Michael into his office. "Lady Humphry and I are going to make a three-year trip through Europe and Asia," he announced. "Our purpose is to advance science. We'll be calling on such greats as André Marie Ampère, Gay Lussac—and even Alesandro Volta."

"What about the war, Sir Humphry? Europe is a tub of acid."

"I know—" Davy lifted his hands impatiently. "Still, Napoleon respects science—as do all crowned heads. Keep in mind that France gave me a gold medal in 1807. Bonaparte has already agreed to issue me a passport. Better yet, he has agreed to provide others for those who will be going with me." He hesitated while he drummed a tattoo on the table with his nails.

With eyes boring into Michael, he said, "Mr. Faraday, Lady Davy and I want you to go with us. You will be my assistant. I will count on you to help with experiments and to assist me when I give public lectures. What do you say?"

"It w-would be a marvelous opportunity," stammered Michael, his mouth suddenly dry. "But what about my job with the Institute?"

"You will have to resign, of course. But I'm quite certain they'll hire you back when we return."

"I'm overwhelmed," replied Michael. He shifted his feet nervously and rubbed his hands together. "Nevertheless, before I give you my answer I think I should consult my mother and—and pray about it."

"Yes, of course. That is the correct thing to do. I would not be happy otherwise." He tapped the desk with his nails again. "However, we will be leaving London on October the 13th!"

11

THE FACE OF
ADVENTURE

"We'll miss you, Michael," said Mrs. Faraday. "Still the chance to see Europe and study with the world's greatest scientist is a great one. Yer Pa would have been mighty proud if he had knowed you had sich a chance. But Michael, my son, I want you to make me some solemn promises—"

"Yes, Ma."

"I want you to promise me that you won't be a-runnin' after any girls, that you will always dress warm, and that you'll stay close to the Lord."

"You don't need to worry about anything, Ma. Girls don't interest me. I'd much rather spend my time with a test tube than a girl! And as far as staying close to the Lord is concerned, have no worry. Like Sir Isaac Newton, I feel I'm just following the footsteps of the Eternal."

Davy was so nervous, he paced back and forth as Michael closed the door of the study. "I have a problem," he said, "It's about my valet. He was all set to go. We had his passport. Then his wife objected. "Would—would you be willing to work in that capacity for a short time?"

"Anything you say, Sir Humphry," replied Michael. He tried to keep any sound of disappointment out of his voice.

"I'll keep your chores to the absolute minimum and when we get to Paris, I'll hire a French valet. The French are good at that sort of thing."

With a notebook handy, Michael mounted the carriage that would take them to Plymouth. He sat next to the coachman. Excitedly, he made notes of everything of interest. Early the next morning, he jotted his impressions in the notebook:

> I have never before left London at a greater distance than twelve miles and now I leave it perhaps for many years. . . . 'Tis a strange venture at this time to trust ourselves in a foreign and hostile country. . . . If we return safe the pleasures of recollection will be highly enhanced by the dangers encountered.

The first hazard Michael faced was not entirely unexpected. Rumors had already indicated that Lady Davy could be difficult. Soon these rumors were confirmed. Again and again she summoned him at their overnight stops along the way and snarled complaints in her high, I'm-your-superior voice. The tune and the content of her song seldom varied. One moment it was, "Michael, these sheets are simply shocking! I insist that they be ironed again." An hour later she would insist that the floor be swept. Sometimes, she would half-scream, "Michael, the bath water isn't hot enough." Once she demanded that they change hotels.

At Plymouth, the carriage was taken apart and loaded on the ship that was to transport them across the channel. Thinking the sea too rough, Lady Davy insisted on remaining in Plymouth an extra day. "I get so frightfully seasick," she complained.

The moment the Davy party unloaded at Morlaix, all were detained by the French authorities. The stern-looking officers were not satisfied with their passports. "This is most unusual!" exclaimed one, his fists doubled. "We will check with Paris. In the meantime, you will remain here."*

Six or seven days later, clearance was finally received, and they continued on to Paris. Lady Davy didn't like the primitive roads. But even though she seethed like a volcano, she could do nothing about it. French hotels were also a shock. At one place they were preceded through the "hotel door" by a horse! Even Michael was horrified. About French food, he was extremely graphic:

> On the right hand of the passage . . . is the kitchen. Here a fire of wood is generally surrounded by idlers, beggars, or nondescripts of the town who meet to warm themselves and chatter with the mistress. . . . I think it is impossible for an English person to eat the things that come out of this place except through ignorance . . . and oppressive hunger.

The scientists in Paris were ready for Sir Humphry.

---

*Unknown to the Davy party, Napoleon was fighting—and losing—the Battle of the Nations at this time. Fought at Leipzig, Germany, the French lost 60,000 men.

The moment he registered, they came to visit and lionize him. When not needed, Michael wandered through the city viewing the sights. He made it a point to visit the Place de la Concorde where Lavoisier had been executed. As he viewed the dreadful spot where so many had lost their lives during the Reign of Terror, he recalled the words of Lagrange who, when referring to Lavoisier, had said, "Only a moment to cut off that head, and another hundred years may not give us another like it!"

Michael liked what could be seen in the city, even though he was wary of the small businessmen.

> I am quite out of patience with the infamous exorbitance of these Parisians. They seem to have neither sense of honesty nor shame in their dealings. They will ask you twice the value of a thing with as much coolness as if they were going to give it to you. . . . It would seem that every tradesman here is a rogue unless they have different meanings for words than we have.

So determined was Michael to widen his education, he even recorded the actual measurements of the museums, public buildings, and libraries which he visited! He also made lists of their contents.

While strolling near the French Upper House, he was startled at seeing Napoleon being driven up in a carriage. Dressed in full uniform, the emperor apparently was on his way to the Upper House to make a speech. Excitedly, Michael wrote:

> He was sitting in one corner of his carriage, covered and almost hidden from sight by an enormous robe of ermine, and his face overshadowed by a tremendous plume of feathers that descended from a velvet hat. The distance was too great to distinguish the features well, but he seemed of

dark countenance and somewhat corpulent. His carriage was very rich and fourteen servants stood upon it in various parts.

On returning to the hotel after several hours of study in the museums, Michael found Davy in earnest conversation with Ampère and several other prominent French scientists. Davy introduced Michael to them. He was acquainted with the accomplishments of all of them, but he was particularly attracted to Ampére because of his work in electricity. Also, he remembered that his father had been guillotined in the Reign of Terror.

After the distinguished guests were gone, Davy's excitement flamed upward. It was as if someone had suddenly turned on the gas to its widest opening. "Look what they brought me!" he said. He handed Michael a small vial containing bluish-black flakes with a metallic gleam.

"What is it?" asked Michael.

"No one knows. So far the French are calling it *Substance X.*"

Davy unlocked his portable laboratory and selected a pair of glass tubes. "Let's see if we can find out just what it is," he said. He was about to remove a few flakes for testing when he noticed that the vial was filling with a violet-colored vapor. "That's strange," he muttered, half to himself. "The mere heat of my hand has made it vaporize!"

He placed the vial in the opened window and within moments the vapor subsided and was replaced with the same sort of flakes or crystals which they had seen in the beginning.

After handing a few crystals to Michael, he said, "Put them in the tube and fill it with water; and while you're doing that, I'll mix some with alcohol in my tube."

The water had no apparent effect, but the alcohol turned dark brown.

While studying the discolored alcohol in the light streaming through the window, Davy murmured, "I wish we had a strong voltaic battery."

"Should I get you one?" asked Michael.

"Yes, go to M. Chevreul's laboratory at the Jarden des Plantes. He has a very strong one and I'm sure he'll lend it to us."

As Michael headed toward the laboratory, he could not keep from chuckling. This was because he had heard the story explaining why Chevreul had such a strong battery. Annoyed that others had succeeded in decomposing alkalies before the French, Napoleon had demanded the reason why.

"The reason is because we have not built a voltaic battery of sufficient power," was the prompt answer.

"Then," exclaimed the emperor, "let one be instantly formed without regard to either cost or labor!"

After the battery was completed, Napoleon went to the laboratory to see—and test it. Before anyone could warn him, he impulsively placed the terminals under his tongue. The resulting shock almost knocked him unconscious. Upon recovery, the emperor stomped out of the building without uttering a sound. Horrified, the witnessing scientists were also silent.

The battery with which Michael returned consisted of twenty-four double plates immersed in a solution of muriate of ammonia together with a little nitric acid. Testing it for power, Davy found the battery produced a fat spark.

Again and again Sir Humphry applied the electrical

energy to the crystals; and although he tried every way he could imagine, he was unable to separate anything from the crystals. This proved, he believed, that Substance X was an element!

With fingers itching to record his discovery, Davy addressed a letter to the Royal Society. In this letter, dated Paris, December 10, 1813, he said, ". . . from all the facts that have been stated, there is every reason to consider this new substance as *an undecompounded body.*" By undecompounded body he clearly meant element. He called the new element *iodine.* Somewhat later, French chemists named it *iode* because of the color of its violate vapor.°

Michael, delighted that he had witnessed this great discovery, wrote in his journal:

> The discovery of this substance in matters so common and supposed so well known must be a stimulus of no small force to the enquiring minds of modern chemists. It is a proof of the imperfect state of the science even in these parts considered as completely understood. It is an earnest of the plentiful reward that awaits the industrious cultivator of this the most extensive branch of experimental knowledge."

Michael was ecstatic at having been a co-witness to this monumental discovery. Still, he was annoyed that Sir Humphry had gotten so involved he had forgotten to employ a valet!

On December 29, the party headed south. The fact

°The original crystals came from the ashes of seaweed, discovered by the French chemist Bernard Courtois. The French were annoyed at Davy for claiming to have identified iodine as an element. They gave the credit to Joseph Gay-Lussac.

that England was at war with France did not seem to frighten Michael. Indeed, he did not even seem to think about it. While in Montpellier on January 8, it did not occur to him that the inhabitants of this southern French city were feverishly preparing to resist an expected invasion by the armies of the Duke of Wellington who had just defeated the Napoleonic forces in Spain.

With a carefree attitude, Michael casually entered a fort.

> I entered it and after winding along some dark passages came out into the open space within. The stroll round the ramparts was pleasant but I imagine that at times while enjoying myself I was transgressing, for the sentinels regarded me sharply and more particularly, at least I thought so, as I stood looking at one corner where for some cause or other the fortifications were injured.

The fact that he was not shot, or at least arrested, can only be explained as a near-miracle.

While in France, Michael acquired a working knowledge of French—a language with which Sir Humphry was already familiar. Michael even learned to read and write it.

On February 7, the group began a tedious journey to Italy by way of Nice. Since the winter weather was unusually severe, it was impossible to pull the carriage over the highest passes in the Alps. At one place where the snow was twenty feet deep, the carriage had to be taken apart and carried by porters. No record relates how Lady Davy made the trip. A reasonable guess is that she was carried in a sedan chair. Michael and Sir Humphry walked.

As the two men trudged along, they got to know one

another better. Michael soon discovered that like himself, Sir Humphry had been deeply influenced by a Quaker. This Quaker, Robert Dunkin, had given up his profession as a saddlemaker in order to build scientific instruments.

"He is the one who first interested me in science," explained Davy as he rested at the top of a pass.

As Europe's foremost scientist, Michael was surprised that Davy was not entirely free from superstition. Each time they stopped at an inn to eat, Michael had to make certain that he did not allow his knife and fork to form a cross on his plate. Sir Humphry had a horror of this and insisted that it not be done. Indeed this superstition was so deep, Davy made certain that everyone eating at his table understood it. Michael tried tactfully to learn the reason for this superstition, but he was not successful.

At Genoa they visited an aquarium and studied some electric eels that had recently arrived from the Amazon. "They have three sets of batteries," said Davy, pointing to a group of the snakelike creatures. "Their most powerful one is strong enough to stun a horse. The other two are weak. It is quite possible that they use these for communication."

"And what are their batteries like?" asked Michael, leaning forward.

"Like a voltaic battery. About eighty percent of an eel consists of plates placed on top of each other. Perhaps it was from the eel that Professor Galvani got his idea about animal electricity."

Davy borrowed a few electric fish and tried to separate oxygen and hydrogen from water with their current. The experiment was not conclusive. "They're just too small and weak," he muttered.

While in Milan, Davy introduced Michael to Professor Volta, now in his sixty-fifth year. Esctatic with this opportunity, Michael wrote that Volta was a "hale and elderly man, bearing the red ribbon, and very free in conversation." Michael considered this visit with him to be the highlight of the trip.

At Florence, Davy summoned Faraday to his room. "The Grand Duke of Tuscany has offered me the use of his magnifying glass for an experiment," he said. "As you may know, it is three-and-a-half feet across. We will focus the rays of the sun on a diamond and see what happens. It—"

"Lavoisier did that many years ago," cut in Michael excitedly. "He found that when air was excluded from the diamonds they did not burn. They were merely discolored, and that only slightly. This was so even though his lense was four feet across—"

"True, Mr. Faraday. But my experiment will be radically different. Instead of excluding oxygen from the diamond, we will withdraw all of the air and replace it with pure oxygen!"

"Pure oxygen?" questioned Michael, his eyes widening. "If you do that the diamond will be completely burned." He shuddered. "It will probably turn into pure carbon. And if it does that, Sir Humphry, what will it prove?"

"If the diamond turns into pure carbon, it may prove a lot." Suddenly Davy was so excited he began to pace back and forth. "If a diamond can be changed into carbon, what will stop us from changing carbon into diamonds?"

"Wouldn't we be trying to do the impossible? Sir Isaac Newton tried to make gold and failed."

"Not at all. If a diamond is pure carbon it is merely another form of the same element, just as ice is another form of water."

As the audience watched, Sir Humphry focused the rays of the sun onto the diamond. From the three-and-a-half-foot glass the rays passed through a three-inch convex lens. At first nothing happened. Indeed, some of the people lost interest. But at the end of forty-five minutes the precious stone became opaque and then it began to burn with a fantastic ruby-red color.

Overcome with excitement, the people leaped to their feet and gave a mighty cheer.

With his usual dramatic skill, Davy explained what had happened. Then, to prove his point, he removed a portion of the carbon dioxide and asked Michael to place it within a bottle of limewater. This done, the limewater turned a milky color, proving that the gas produced by the burning diamond was pure carbon dioxide.

Davy's next experiment was to focus the sun onto a lump of pure graphite. Having done this, and after excluding the water vapor, he again had what he considered to be pure carbon dioxide. Before this experiment, Sir Humphry had been inclined to believe that graphite was a compound of hydrogen and diamond. Now he was utterly convinced that diamonds, charcoal, and graphite are all forms of the same thing—carbon. This conviction firmed his belief that someday diamonds could be manufactured.[*]

---

[*] On February 15, 1955, General Electric announced that they had succeeded in producing diamonds. They had accomplished this breakthrough by subjecting graphite to a pressure of 1,500,000 pounds per square inch while heating it at 5,000° F.

Again, having assisted in an experiment that proved a new scientific fact, Michael felt a strong sense of pride. He enjoyed Florence, especially for its historical value. He visited the place where Savonarola was burned; the home of the poet, Dante; and the museum which displayed the telescope used by Galileo to discover four of Jupiter's many moons in 1610. This telescope was made from a pipe removed from a discarded pipe organ.

But in spite of the excitement of Florence, Michael was getting weary. Although less than a year had passed, he was already homesick for London. He missed his family and friends in the Sandemanian congregation such as Mr. and Mrs. Deacon, George Leighton, Miss Cumacher—and especially the Barnards. Mr. Barnard, an elder in the church, was a silversmith—and the most prosperous member of the church. The Barnards and Faradays had been friends for as long as Michael could remember. Now, while cleaning and polishing Davy's apparatus, he thought of them.

The two sons, George and Edward, had been Michael's playmates. George, the oldest, was studying to be an artist. During Michael's visits to museums in France and Italy, he thought of him. Standing in front of Michaelangelo's David, he almost felt guilty that George wasn't by his side.

There were three Barnard girls. The oldest was already married. Michael knew the other two best. Sarah, the middle one, was ten years younger than Michael. Still, they'd had a lot of fun together. Now, often bored with his work, he remembered her blue eyes, firm chin, and the dark curls she sported over her ears.

At the time he had sailed from Plymouth, Jane was not yet ten. Nevertheless, he had had a fine time teasing her.

From Florence, Sir Humphry and the group went to Rome. Miachel made notes on the Colosseum, the manner in which the ancient bridges were constructed, the Vatican, and other points of interest. But as famous as these places were, he was tired.

From Rome the party went north to Geneva, and then again they all returned to Rome. Now, even the most famous spots in the Eternal City seemed dull. Michael vented some of his frustration in a long letter to Benjamin Abbott:

> Alas! how foolish perhaps to leave home, to leave those whom I loved and who loved me for a time uncertain in its length, but certainly long and which may perhaps stretch out into eternity! And what are the boasted advantages to be gained? Knowledge. Yes, knowledge but what knowledge? Knowledge of the world, of men, of manners, of books, and of languages. . . . Alas! how degrading it is to be learned when it places us on a level with rogues and scoundrels! . . . Ah, Ben, I am not sure that I have acted wisely in leaving a pure and certain enjoyment for such a pursuit.

Between the lines, one can feel the pressures exerted by Lady Davy. Not only did she consider him a servant, but she let him know it in many ways. Seldom was he allowed to dine with them—even when they were guests in a distinguished home. On such occasions, she insisted that he eat with the servants!

In another letter Michael was more pointed: "She is haughty and proud to an excessive degree and delights in making her inferiors feel her power."

Each time Sir Humphry mentioned a new place he hoped to visit, Michael shuddered. Turkey sounded exotic, but he was far too weary to be excited.

Late in January, word reached them that the last battle of the War of 1812 had been fought on January 8. It was named the Battle of New Orleans. Michael was delighted that Britain and the United States were at peace. And yet he reflected that the peace treaty had been signed the previous Christmas Eve. Had faster communications been available, this battle would not have been fought.

This American news had no effect on Davy. Another story did. Early in March the newspapers headlined that Napoleon along with 1,050 men had escaped from Elba on February 26. Soon it was learned that he had landed at Cannes, was heading for Paris, and was gathering an army on the way.

Deeply concerned, Davy switched from experiments to following headlines. "Perhaps Napoleon will be arrested before he gets to Paris," he said. But Davy's hopes were not fulfilled. Declaring himself loyal to Louis XVIII, Marshal Ney gathered a force of six thousand and headed south to arrest his former commander. "I will bring Napoleon back in an iron cage," he boasted to the king.

Ney's boast was an empty one, for when he saw his old chieftain he was overwhelmed. Throwing his arms around Napoleon in an affectionate embrace, he joined forces with him. Learning this, Davy thumped the newspaper on the table while he exclaimed, "This means that all of Europe will be in flames again. We have no alternative. We must return to London—and at once!"

While in Brussels on April 16, Michael wrote to his mother telling her he "hoped" to be home in three days. After he had mailed the letter, it suddenly occurred to him that when he reached London he would be unemployed. That grim fact pushed much of the joy of anticipation from his heart. What would he do?

12

NEW WORLDS

As Michael climbed the steps to his home in Weymouth Street, he was so excited he forgot that he was nearly penniless and unemployed.

After everyone was exhausted from welcoming him back, Mrs. Faraday remarked, "Yer letter from Brussels said you'd be home in about three days. That would have been April 19! You should have seen the big dinner we prepared for you on the 20th. Since you didn't come, we ate it. Now it's Sunday, the 23rd; and this means that we must go to church. We'll have our meal with the congregation."

"That suits me fine," said Michael.

With a hand on his shoulder and a curious look in her eyes, Mrs. Faraday said, "Since you've seen all them big cathedrals you may not be happy with our little church.

We don't have no big colored-glass windows and lots of our people can't read—"

"Those things don't make any difference to me," said Michael. "What counts is if a man knows God's laws—and follows them!"

Following another shower of kisses, Michael sank into his pew to enjoy the services. The congregation seemed smaller than before. Wondering who might be missing, he slowly looked around. They were all there, all thirty of them. The only absentees were Mr. and Mrs. Deacon, and he had already learned that they had gone to Dundee for a visit.

Michael reasoned that the crowd merely seemed smaller because he had become accustomed to the throngs that were attracted to Davy's lectures. As he smiled at the people he noticed they had changed. Older members had become grayer, middle-aged ones fatter, the children taller. A shy glance at Sarah Barnard revealed that she had blossomed into a young woman.

As the elder preached, Michael suddenly became aware of the stooped man's bad grammar. And then, his mind wandering, he began to think of his own problems. After he resigned from the Royal Institution to accompany Davy, the directors had hired an assistant porter to take his place. If not an insult, this fact seemed to prove that they didn't think much of his work. That he could be replaced by an assistant porter was a chilling thought.

Glancing at his mother and Meg sitting beside her, he was acutely aware that he was now responsible for their support. What if he couldn't get a job? Or what if the government tried to draft him into Wellington's army to fight Napoleon? With such thoughts hammering his brain, he scrunched lower and lower in his pew.

Nearly sick with apprehension, Michael forced himself to listen to the elder. "As everyone knows," preached this man who earned his living sweeping the streets, "us Sandemanians don't have no insurance. And why is that? It's because Jesus said: 'Take no thought for your life, what ye shall eat, or what ye shall drink; nor yet for your body, what ye shall put on. Is not the life more than meat, and the body than raiment? Behold the fowls of the air: for they sow not, neither do they reap, nor gather into barns; yet your heavenly Father feedeth them. Are ye not much better than they?' (Matthew 6:25, 26).

"Now all of you know I've been out of work many times. Once or twice me and wife have been worse off than Old Mother Hubbard, for we didn't even have no bone fer ourselves let alone a dog. Yet, we never starved. Why? 'Cause God keers for His own!"

As Michael listened, he slowly pushed himself erect in the pew. Although this nearly illiterate elder had no knowledge of Newton's laws and had never heard of John Dalton's revolutionary atomic theory, nevertheless, it was obvious that the man understood some of God's basic laws. Suddenly Michael was dabbing at his eyes. Yes, it was a joy to be a Sandemanian!

On May 7 Michael was summoned to the Royal Institution. Eagerly he presented himself at the appointed time. "We are glad you're back in London," said the director. "Your name was brought up in our last meeting and we have a new job for you. How would you like to be Superintendent of the Apparatus of the Laboratory and Mineralogical Collection?"

"That's a long title—"

"But would you like the job?"

"Of course!"

"All right, the job is yours. From now on your pay will be thirty shillings a week. This is five shillings more than you received before."

"Will I h-have the use of my old room?" asked Michael trying to keep excitement from edging his voice.

"Certainly. The room will be free and we will supply your candles. All of them. And from what I've heard you burn a lot of candles!"

Had it not been that he had reached the dignified age of twenty-four, and was afraid he might be watched, Michael would have run all the way home. As it was, he merely took big steps.

"It's the hand of the Lord!" exclaimed Mrs. Faraday as she led Michael to her favorite chair. "We must kneel and thank Him right now."

"And do you know what I'm going to do with the extra five shillings?" asked Michael.

"I have no idea."

"I'm going to pay Meg's tuition to a good school!"

During Michael's first weeks at the Royal Institution, Davy was gone most of the time. Lecturing in his place was a professor of chemistry, William T. Brande—a kindly gentleman with a high forehead, curly hair, and side-whiskers. One of Michael's jobs was to prepare the apparatus for his lectures and to assist him while he gave them.

Brande knew his chemistry, but he lacked Davy's fire. The result of this was that the lecture attendance went down. And since the R.I. depended on lecture fees for a large part of their income, the directors became concerned. Indeed, things became so bad that the fuel bill for 1816 could not be paid until 1818. To help the Institute's influence, Brande edited the *Quarterly Journal of Science*. This unofficial journal helped the R.I. remain in contact with a host of friends, and many of these friends contributed money.

Michael helped Brande in this editorial work. It was a task he enjoyed immensely, for it gave him an excuse to spend countless hours in the Institute's well-stocked library.

From the beginning of his new job, Michael determined to review the history of chemistry from the end of the 1700s until the present time. One of his methods was to take a book apart, and to insert blank sheets between all the pages. On these blank pages he added his own personal notes. Having filled them, he rebound the book. Among the volumes he treated this way were those of Professor Brande.

So busy was Michael with his various tasks he wrote to Abbott: "Friday is my only spare evening this week." While doing this research, he was amazed at the contributions made to science by dissenters. For example, there was John Dalton whose atomic theory was to shake the entire concept of chemistry.

Born to Quaker parents in a tiny village three miles from Cockermouth° in 1759, he faced the usual problems confronting dissenters. One of the most serious of these was that he was barred from the universities by the same law that barred Roman Catholics and Jews. Because of this *conformity legislation*—enacted in the early 1660s—

°This city—250 miles northwest of London—was also the birthplace of Fletcher Christian, mutineer on the *Bounty* in 1789.

dissenters were forced to found their own schools of higher learning. In a way, this was an advantage, for frequently the dissenting academies were better than the conformist schools.

Son of a poor weaver, John Dalton attended a Quaker academy at Pardshaw. He so admired the teacher, John Fletcher, that when he left Dalton founded a school of his own even though he was only twelve or thirteen. Thus his formal education was not much more than that of Michael Faraday. While studying under Fletcher, Dalton learned the value of determination. Once, when confronted with a difficult problem, he replied in his Cumbrian dialect, "*I can't deu't to-neet, but mebby to-morn I will.*" Splashes of this dialect stayed with him the rest of his life.

Although the school he founded was not a success, he used every spare moment to cram more knowledge into his head. Finding an article he liked, he copied it word for word. Curious about science, he corresponded with such men as Benjamin Franklin. When he was able to afford a telescope, he studied the stars and planets—and filled books with notes. Indeed, he became so interested in learning that he and a few friends founded a book club! The main purpose of the club, of course, was so that he would have more books to read.

Soon he began writing articles for magazines, and these articles spread his fame as a master of knowledge. On the basis of his soaring reputation, he got a job as an assistant teacher at the Quaker school in Kendal.

While at Kendal, John bought a pair of stockings for his mother. After thanking him, she remarked, "They are fine stockings, John, but since they are cherry red I cannot wear them to meeting. Remember we're Quakers."

"They're not red, Ma. They're blue!"

In this fashion John Dalton learned that he was color blind.° He was thus shocked to discover that things were not what they had seemed during the previous twenty-seven years. This fact pushed him to study even harder. After numerous teaching and lecturing experiences, Dalton suggested to William Johns, a dissenting minister in Manchester, that he house and feed him as a guest. The pastor agreed that this was a good idea and led him to the spare bedroom. Dalton promptly moved in and stayed for nearly thirty years!

Michael was chuckling over the similarities between Dalton and himself when he heard footsteps. Lifting his head, he faced Professor Brande. "What's the matter?" he asked, noticing the unusual brightness in the chemist's face.

"What day is it, Mr. Faraday?" asked Brande, excitedly.

"It is Tuesday, June 20, 1815. Why do you ask, sir?"

"Haven't you heard the news?" demanded Brande, staring at him.

"What news?" Michael looked startled.

Brande lifted his brows in amazement. "Where have you been?"

"I was in church on Sunday, and I've been here the rest of the time." Michael pointed to three stacks of books.

"This is amazing. Absolutely amazing. While you were in church on Sunday evening Napoleon was crushed by Wellington and Blücher at Waterloo. This means the Na-

---

°Since he published a paper on the subject, color blindness was dubbed Daltonism.

poleonic Wars are over! We are now living in a new world. June 18 will be one of the great dates of history."

After a silence, Michael said, "Professor Brande, maybe you can tell me something. How did that Quaker Dalton ever conceive of the atomic theory? It's so complicated."

Brande cocked his head to one side as he stared at Faraday. After a painful moment, he said, "Weren't you in Brussels on April 16?"

"Yes, I was there with Sir Humphry Davy."

"Don't you know that Waterloo is only ten miles southeast of Brussels? Just think, Mr. Faraday, you were within ten miles of the place only two months ago!" Brande was so animated he thumped the desk with his fist.

"That is remarkable," conceded Michael. "But do tell me, Professor Brande, how did a poverty-stricken Quaker like Dalton ever work out the atomic theory?"

"You are a most extraordinary person, Mr. Faraday! Here we've witnessed one of the great events of history, and yet all that interests you is science." He shook his head. Then a wide smile crossed his face. "I'll tell you how he worked out that theory. He studied day and night just like you—"

"Seriously, professor, how did he do it?"

"You've asked a difficult question! Dalton is an intellectual giant. But like Newton, he has learned to stand on the shoulders of others. As you know, he lectured here at the R.I. in 1803. While he was here, it was learned that he had copied down a section from Newton's *Opticks* that bears on that subject." Brande pulled a book from a top shelf, and searched for the desired passage. "Ah, here it is." Moving close to Michael, he read:

> It seems probable to me that God in the beginning formed matter in solid, massy, hard, impenetrable, moving particles of such size and figures, and with such other properties, and in such proportion to space as most conducted to the end for which He formed them. . . .
>
> God is able to create particles of matter of several sizes and figures, and in several proportions to the space they occupy, and perhaps of different densities and forces.

"But Sir Isaac did not understand the atomic theory," said Michael. "Indeed, I think he was mistaken about light—"

"Of course Newton didn't understand the atomic theory as Dalton has proclaimed it. Nevertheless, his great mind leaned in that direction. There is nothing completely new about the conception of atoms. The Greek philosopher, Democritus, speculated that the world is made up of tiny balls. He called them *atomoi*. And please remember that he lived between four and five centuries before Christ!"

"I'm still amazed at Dalton's conception of atoms. Perhaps sometime I'll be able to meet him. I'd like to learn how he studies—"

"His favorite way to think through a problem is to sit in a chair with a cat on one knee and a newspaper on the other," said Brande with a laugh. "But like the rest of us, Dalton is not always right. As you may know, he wrote a book on English grammar. In it, he defined *phenomenon* as a *masculine* noun and *phenomena* as a *feminine* noun!"

Michael enjoyed this conversation even though he had already made thorough notes on all that Brande had had to say. Indeed, he had already chuckled over the cat and grammar stories!

During these busy years, Michael had no thoughts about marriage. From firsthand experience, he had seen the misery endured by Sir Humphry Davy because of his marriage.° Moreover, two of his heroes, John Dalton and Isaac Watts, had remained single and he did not see why he should not do the same. Just as Prime Minister William Pitt claimed to be married to his country, he felt he was married to science.

In his *Common Place Book* Michael jotted down in poetry what he thought of marriage. The long poem begins with a shattering verse:

> What is the pest and plague of human life? And what the curse that often brings a wife? 'Tis Love.

One afternoon while visiting with Edward Barnard, he showed him this poem. Edward read it through twice and then smiled mysteriously. "Do you really believe that?" he asked.

In reply, Michael laughed and snapped the book shut.

As the weeks and months passed by Michael was so busy he wished each week had eight days instead of seven. Even so, he never neglected the church services. He had a fine baritone voice and spent many happy hours teaching the congregation to sing.

Because of the industrial revolution, coal mining was becoming more and more important in Great Britain. The new steam engines had insatiable appetites for coal. Because of this demand owners and operators became

---

°Regarding Davy's marriage, Sir Walter Scott wrote: "She has a temper and Davy has a temper, and their two tempers are not of one temper and they quarrel like cat and dog."

more and more inhuman. As their greed increased, working time was pushed to twelve hours a day, six days a week. Likewise, women, together with six-year-olds—and sometimes younger—were employed in the depths of the mines.

Even more hazardous in the mines than the grueling working hours, the employment of women and children, improper ventilation, and inadequate timber support, were explosions set off by the flames in miners' lamps. Such explosions often killed hundreds. Following a long series of accidents, Sir Humphry Davy was urgently contacted and asked to invent a safety lamp.

Upon returning from a hunting trip in the Highlands, Davy approached Michael Faraday in early October 1815. "I want you to help me develop a lamp that will be safe in the mines—one that won't ignite firedamp." He pointed to several containers filled with samples of the explosive gas. In as serious a tone as Michael had ever heard him use, he added: "One way or another we must find a method to keep a light burning within that stuff without exploding it. This means we must do a lot of experimenting!"

13

IN LOVE!

Michael kept busy doing assignments in the laboratory while Davy sought clues to the firedamp problem. With an uncanny feel for chemistry, Sir Humphry found that firedamp did not ignite as readily as mixtures of air with hydrogen, carbonic oxide, or even coal gas.

Following these experiments, Davy studied the expansive power of various mixes when they were exploded. From this study he found a clue to the ultimate solution. The clue was that a flame from a mixture of coal gas and air took an entire second to pass through a foot-long pipe with an inside diameter of a quarter of an inch.

"This is great," he muttered, "for coal gas is even more inflammable than firedamp!"

Next, Davy discovered that the flame from this same mixture could not pass through a pipe with an inside diameter of one-seventh of an inch. His excitement increasing, he ignited a jar of firedamp which was joined by an aperture one-sixth of an inch in diameter to a bladder filled with firedamp. Although the jar of firedamp burned vigorously, the firedamp in the bladder remained undisturbed. Davy was delighted.

Additional experiment proved, as one biographer has noted, "that the explosion would not pass through metal troughs or slots if their diameter was less than one seventh of an inch (that is) if they were of sufficient length. Nor would it pass through fine wire gauze."

With this information, Sir Humphry designed a safety lamp which, with improvements, is still in use. When John Buddle suggested that Davy take out a patent, he shook his head. "I never thought of such a thing," he protested. "My sole object was to serve the cause of humanity; and if I have succeeded, I am amply rewarded."

Michael was impressed. He realized that Sir Humphry had turned down a source of vast income. He resolved that in similar circumstances he would do the same.

Early in 1820, Meg—now a young lady of eighteen—approached Michael just after the church meal. "Let's go for a walk," she said.

As they headed toward Bunhill Fields, Michael said, "By the tone of your voice you sound as if you have something on your mind—"

"I have! Michael it won't be long until you're thirty."

"So?"

"So why don't you get married?"

"Married!" Michael pointed to the grave of Isaac Watts. "He didn't get married and look at all that he accomplished." Flipping a hand in the direction of Wesley

Chapel across City Road, he added, "Look at all the trouble John Wesley's wife caused him—"

"Yes, but John married a widow! Besides, his brother Charles had a happy marriage—and he wrote 6,000 hymns."

Michael smiled. "I've just been so busy I haven't had time to think of marriage. Also, who would I ever marry? And who would have me with my odd-shaped head?"

"Don't be silly, Michael. I've watched those gray eyes of yours pausing at the Barnard pew. And I agree. Sarah is a mighty fine girl!"

The idea of marriage was new to Faraday. But like Galileo when he first viewed Jupiter through a telescope, he began to spend time studying the subject. Analyzing the phenomenon of love brought him face-to-face with a major problem. "How do you know if a girl will marry you?" he inquired of Meg.

"Oh, that's quite simple. You just take her to some secluded spot and, when you're alone, ask her."

This reply seemed reasonable enough and so Michael began to take Sarah for long walks. Again and again he intended to bring up the subject of marriage, but each time he didn't quite manage it. Once, just as the words of a proposal were forming in his heart, Sarah grew cold and aloof. "I have a question," she said, her voice as cold as the eyes of a frozen fish.

"Let's hear it," replied Michael, slightly alarmed.

Taking her hand from his, she said, "What is the meaning of a poem that begins: 'What is the pest and plague of human life? And what the curse that often brings a wife? 'Tis Love'?"

"Well, I-I—" He was silent for a dozen steps. "Sarah, where did you read that?"

"My brother Edward told me he read it in your *Common Place Book*. It was in your own handwriting!"

In response to this, Michael began writing letter after letter to Sarah. In one of them he said, "You know me as well or better than I do myself. You know my former prejudices, and my present thoughts—you know my weaknesses, my vanity, my whole mind; you have converted me from one erroneous way, let me hope you will correct what others are wrong."

Alarmed, Sarah showed the letter to her father. Understanding human nature, Mr. Barnard reasoned that Michael Faraday was merely love-sick. His cure was to separate the two by sending Sarah to Ramsgate—a seaside town southeast of London.

While this drama was being enacted, a Danish professor, Dr. Hans Christian Oersted°—his PhD was from the University of Copenhagen—was unknowingly about to perform an experiment that would revolutionize the science of electricity.

While lecturing to a group of advanced students during the spring of 1820, Oersted accidentally placed a platinum wire carrying electricity close to and parallel with the magnetic needle of a compass. When he did this, the needle twitched. Puzzled, he frowned. He was intrigued, but not concerned enough to perform other related experiments right then. Instead, he shrugged and went ahead with his previously planned lecture.

Several weeks later, Oersted procured a larger battery

°He was a close friend of the author, Hans Christian Andersen. Indeed, Oersted helped support him during his lean years. On a certain day each week Andersen dined in his home for more than a quarter of a century.

and repeated the "accidental" experiment. He now discovered that the twitch of the needle was reversed when the flow of current was reversed, or if the current-bearing wire was placed beneath the needle. Believing he had discovered a new princple, he prepared a four-page tract in Latin and mailed it to the scientists of Europe. The tract was titled: *Experimenta circa effectum conflictus electrici in acum magneticam*—"Experiements on the Effects of a Current of Electricity (or Electrical Conflict) on the Magnetic Needle."

The tract produced a sensation. Excitedly Ampère and others repeated Oersted's experiments and tried to explain the results.

In time, Faraday learned of the breakthrough; but since he was concentrating on chemistry plus the winning of Sarah, he paid little attention. True, when Davy heard about the experiment he rushed into the R.I. and explained what had happened to Faraday and both of them repeated what Oersted had done. That seemed to end the matter.

During the following April, William Hyde Wollaston, a medical doctor turned scientist, stopped at the R.I. to see if he and Davy could perform Oersted's experiment in reverse. Since the Dane had made a magnetic needle turn under the influence of an electric current, Wollaston wondered why he could not make a current-bearing wire turn when influenced by a magnet.

With the hindsight of our time, it is easy to see that neither of the two realized the ultimate significance of what they were attempting to do.

Wollaston and Davy experimented for hours without results. The wire just would not turn. After they had given up, Faraday stepped into the room. Davy then explained what they had been trying to do. Michael, his mind burning with possible new alloys of steel and his work with chlorine, only half listened.

Later, when this incident was almost forgotten, Faraday received a letter from his long-time friend, R. Phillips, requesting that he do an article on this "new branch of science" for the magazine, *Annals of Philosophy*. Michael agreed with reluctance because he had resolved not to write on any subject unless he had first performed all of the necessary experiments.

At the time Michael agreed to do the article, he had no way of knowing that the experiments he would perform to gather his material would make him famous. Nor did he realize that the publication of the results of one of those experiments would all but ruin his career. His real concern at the moment was Sarah!

Michael's separation from Sarah was more than he could bear. Ignoring his better judgment, he boarded a coach and headed for Ramsgate. Unfortunately, he knew more about Dalton's atoms than he did about romance. From his own hand we know how he acted:

> I was in strange spirits and had very little command over myself, though I managed to preserve appearances. I expressed strong disappointment at the look of the town and of the cliffs, I criticized all around me with a malicious tone, and, in fact, was just getting into a humor which would have offended the best-natured person, when I perceived that, unwittingly, I had, for the purpose of disguising hopes which had been raised in me so suddenly, and might have been considered presumptuous, assumed an appearance of general contempt and dislike. The moment I perceived the danger of the path on which I was running, I stopped, and talked of home and friends.

As Michael spoke of home, Sarah began to soften like wax in a burner. He then began to discuss her brother George and his paintings. Michael liked his work, and told her so. Again he noticed that her resistance was disappearing. Before he left for his hotel, he worked up enough courage to make a suggestion.

"Let's go to Dover tomorrow. It's a wonderful place and we'll get to see the coast of France."

The trip to this famous port took less than two hours. Since the coach was half-empty, Michael and Sarah managed to hold hands without embarrassment. That evening, with the sea at their feet and the sun a mass of red in the west, Michael proposed and Sarah accepted.

After some rough calculations on the sand, the wedding date was set for June 12.

Michael's next problem was to find a place to live. Perhaps the R.I. would give them permission to set up housekeeping in the attic of the Institute! Since Sir Humphry had been elected president of the organization the previous November, Michael went to him.

"I'll see what I can do," promised Davy, beating a tattoo on the desk with his nails.

That May permission was granted and Michael was promoted. His new title was Superintendent of the Laboratory. But his salary remained the same—£100 per annum plus heat, candles—and rooms in the Royal Institute attic.

One month after his marriage, Michael Faraday publicly announced his faith in Christ at the Sandemanian Church.

"Why didn't you tell me you were going to do that?" asked Sarah, highly pleased.

"Because it's between God and me," said Michael.

147

14

THE WHIRLING
WIRE

Tormented by R. Phillip's request for an article on the magnetic qualities of electricity, Michael pushed aside his experiments in chemistry to devote himself to a renewed study of electrical phenomena.

Having studied and made notes on the Leyden jar, together with the discoveries of Volta and Galvani, he concentrated on the progress that had been made during the last twenty years. Like himself, he found that many had been interested in the use of electricity to transmit messages.

Curious about the speed of electricity, Giovanni Aldini—a nephew of Galvani—had stretched a wire between the west jetty in the harbor of Calais to Fort-Rouge. Using the sea as a "ground wire" he connected the wire to a "dissected animal" to see how long it would take the current to cross over and make the dead body twitch.

When all wires were in place, Aldini connected them to a voltaic pile composed of eighty plates of silver and zinc. At the precise moment this was done, the dissected animal twitched. Aldini then concluded that electricity travels with "astonishing rapidity."

This 1803 experiment of Aldini widened eyes in the scientific world. By 1809, Dr. Samuel T. von Soemmering, a German physician, was ready with an advanced idea. During the Academy of Science Convention in Munich that year he announced that he was going to send a message 1,000 feet in an instant.

Previous to this announcement, the German doctor had stretched out thirty-five insulated wires 1,000 feet long. At one end, each wire was connected to a gold rod placed in a glass tube filled with a mixture of water and acid. Each of the tubes represented one of twenty-five letters or one of ten numerals.

As the skeptics watched, he sent a current through first one wire and then another. The moment the current reached a tube, gas bubbles rose to the surface. And thus a "telegram" was transmitted. By 1812 the number of needed wires was reduced to twenty-seven and the maximum distance increased to nearly two miles.

With these facts and many technical notes at hand, Michael began to write the "Historical Sketch of Electromagnetism" for R. Phillips to appear in *Annals of Philosophy.* When he was finished with this article in the summer of 1821, he decided to do another for the *Quarterly Journal of Science.* This new one would be on electromagnetic motions.

With the discoveries of Oersted in mind and the

memory of what Wollaston and Davy had unsuccessfully tried to do in the laboratory, he decided to try a variation of the experiment himself. Faraday realized that one of the great problems in getting a current-carrying wire to revolve around a magnet was mechanical. In order that the wire might flow with electricity, it had to be connected to an electrical source at *both* ends and at the same *time*. If the wire was to rotate, this clearly seemed impossible. He was puzzling over this problem when an extremely simple solution presented itself.

Selecting a bolt-like magnet, he stuck it upright into some melted wax on the bottom of a deep basin. When the wax was completely dry, he poured mercury into the basin until just a few inches of the magnet extended above the surface. Next he put a loop on the end of the wire that hopefully would revolve around the magnet. He connected this loop to the loop on the end of a length of wire connected to a battery.

The wire that was to revolve was now slanted into the mercury—an excellent conductor of electricity. Holding his breath, Faraday now connected another wire from the battery source of the mercury. And then it happened. The wire revolved around the magnet!

Dancing up and down, Faraday shouted, "There it goes! There it goes!" It was a great historical event. Michael Faraday had invented the first electric motor. Tingling with excitement, he reversed the process. Again he was successful. This time the magnet revolved around the wire.

By chance, Editor Phillips showed up at the R.I. the next day. "I must show you something," said Michael. He tried to smother the enthusiasm in his voice, but was far from successful.

As the length of wire spun around in the basin, Phillip's eyes unconsciously followed it. "You must publish what you have done," he said firmly.

Michael hesitated.

"Is there any good reason why you should not publish?"

"N-no, not exactly. But since I want to mention Dr. Wollaston, I think I'd better speak to him first. After all, he had a similar idea—"

"But was it the same as yours?" interrupted Phillips.

"I-I really can't say. His basic idea may have been the same as mine. Nevertheless, he tried to get the wire to spin on its *own* axis, while I got mine to spin *around the magnet*."

"That's quite a difference," said Phillips, shrugging. "But one way or another, I want an article."

In later years, Faraday remembered the occasion as vividly as if it had been printed on his brain with indelible ink. "I went to his house to communicate [the results of the experiment] to him, and to ask permission to refer to his views and experiments. Dr. Wollaston was not in town, nor did he return whilst I remained in town."

Since Wollaston was not available, and since the editor's hand was out, Michael finished the article and turned it in. His motto had always been: *Work. Finish. Publish.* Having done so in the past, he followed through.

The article appeared in the October issue of the *Quarterly Journal of Science*. As Michael was showing it to Sarah, he remarked, "I hope it doesn't upset Sir Humphry—"

"And why would it upset him?" questioned Sarah as she refilled his cup with fresh tea.

"Recently a coolness like a breeze from the North Sea has been coming between us and I deeply regret it. Sir Humphry is a great man—one of the greatest. Without him we would not be here! But like the rest of us he has problems. Last year we were opposing witnesses in a lawsuit. It was most unfortunate.

"The case was between a sugar refiner—Severn, King, and Company—and some insurance people. The refiners had a fire and they believed their insurance should pay. But those who wrote the policies claimed that oil was at fault, and that since they had not been informed that there were large quantities of oil in the plant they refused to pay." Michael rubbed his chin and took a generous bite of chocolate cake.

"It was a most interesting case. The main problem was to find the source of the fire. The refiners insisted the fire was caused by sugar. The insurance companies claimed it was caused by oil.

"Davy and Brande, testifying in behalf of the sugar company, insisted that vapor rising from oil heated at 580° F. was not flammable and that therefore the fire was caused by sugar—not oil. Both of them had arrived at this conclusion by testing small quantities of oil. In contrast, I tried out larger quantities of oil and found that its vapor is flammable at 380° and very flammable at 435° F."

"And how was it settled?" asked Sarah.

Michael laughed. "Fortunately for me, the court decided that Severn, King, and Company were not guilty of fraud; and thus the temperature of oil when its vapor becomes flammable had nothing to do with the verdict. Nevertheless, Davy was unhappy that I had contradicted his testimony. In addition, Sarah, my success in getting the wire to rotate was one of the great events in science. It takes a big man not to be affected when his young assistant has so much success!"

"Do you think Davy is that big?"

"Sometimes he is, and sometimes he isn't." Michael got up and paced the room. "That lawsuit business was terrible," he murmured, speaking half to himself. "Still, I think something good will come of it—"

"What do you mean?"

"Well, I developed a new interest in oil. As you know, my brother Robert works in the gas illuminating business. His company makes gas by pouring whale or codfish oil into a red-hot furnace. The gas that is produced is then compressed into metal bottles at about thirty atmospheres."*

Sarah was so startled she almost dropped the teapot. "Do you mean that the gas which lights buildings like ours comes from whale or codfish oil?" she demanded.

"That's exactly what I mean!" laughed Michael.

Within a week of the publication of the article, Michael noted distrustful looks in the eyes of many he had known for years. And on two occasions a trio of men who were having an animated lowtone conversation, were suddenly silent when he approached. In utter distress, he wrote to James Stodart, a collaborator in the work on the alloys of steel.

"You know perfectly well," he wrote from the depths of his heart, "what distress the very unexpected reception of my paper on magnetism has caused me, and you will therefore not be surprised at my anxiety over it."

Michael suggested that Stodart arrange an interview

---

*Approximately 441 pounds per square inch.

between Wollaston and himself. Since nothing came of this, Faraday wrote to Wollaston begging for a meeting in which they could settle the dispute. Wollaston's answer was cold enough to freeze a pig's liver.

"Sir," he wrote, "you seem to me to labor under some misapprehension of the strength of my feelings upon the subject to which you allude.

"As to the opinions which others may have of your conduct, that is your concern, not mine; and if you fully acquit yourself of making any incorrect use of the suggestions of others, it seems to me that you have no occasion to concern yourself much about the matter."

Personally convinced that he was innocent of plagiarism, Faraday pushed the problem from his mind and continued his research project. As the months passed, the tempest calmed and his general acceptance improved. Within a year he was recognized in scientific circles as a first-class chemist.

Early in March 1823, Davy came into the laboratory while Michael was bent over a table covered with an assortment of bottles and tubes. "And what are you doing now?" he asked, his voice vibrant with its old friendliness.

"I've been working with the hydrate of chlorine. You will remember that in 1810 you showed that what had been previously considered pure chlorine was merely a hydrate."

"Yes, of course."

"Since it's cold, I decided to make a new analysis and find exactly what the proportions are." Laying a finger on a sheet of paper, he added, "Here are the results. The crystals were 27.7% chlorine and 72.3% water."

"Very good, Mr. Faraday." Davy started to leave and

then stopped. "Before preparing a paper on this subject, why don't you heat some chlorine in a sealed tube? The results could be interesting!"

"I will do that, sir," said Michael, bending to his work.

Weeks later, Michael prepared more hydrate of chlorine, poured it into a tube whose upper end had been fused shut, and placed it in water that had been heated to 60° F. He studied the tube cautiously for a tense moment. Nothing happened. Then he increased the heat to 100°. Now as he viewed the tube, his heart began to pound. Curious and unexpected changes were taking place. As he watched these changes, his body tingled from one extremity to the other. Gripped with awe, he felt like Moses when he watched the dividing of the Red Sea. After the experiment, he carefully recorded precisely what had happened:

> The tube became filled with a bright yellow atmosphere, and on examination was found to contain two fluid substances: the one about three fourths of the whole, was a faint yellow color, having very much the appearance of water; the remaining fourth was a heavy bright yellow fluid, lying at the bottom of the former, without any apparent tendency to mix with it. As the tube cooled, the yellow atmosphere condensed into more of the yellow fluid. . . .
>
> By putting the hydrate into a bent tube, afterward hermetically sealed, I found it easy . . . to distill the yellow fluid to one end of the tube and to separate it from the remaining portion.

After Faraday had repeated variations of this experiment a number of times, Dr. J. A. Paris breezed into the lab. Aiming his forefinger at the mass of empty tubes on the table, he remarked, "Mr. Faraday, why do you use such dirty equipment?"

Michael was annoyed by the question. It seemed most unfair, especially since Paris was a close friend of Sir Humphry and Sir Humphry was an extremely messy worker. With considerable grit, Michael forced a smile. "I've just been heating some hydrate of chlorine. It seems I've discovered something interesting. As yet, I really don't know what it is."

"I still think you ought to work with clean tubes," replied Paris pontifically. "Otherwise—"

"The gleam of excitement in Michael's eyes may have distracted him.

"Dr. Paris, those tubes were perfectly clean when I started to work. The fact that they are *now* dirty may mean something important."

"If so, let me know what it is," replied Paris over his shoulder as he left the room.

While Michael was frowning at the soiled tubes and considering what he should do, he picked up one that was cooling at the window. Yes, the tube was dirty just as Paris had said—moreover, the dirt had a greasy look. Selecting a sharp file, he cut into the sealed end of the tube. The instant the glass was severed, there was a loud explosion.

Amazed, Michael examined the tube fragments. They were spotless—all of them! Suddenly a wild thought gripped his mind. But before he could accept it, he would have to experiment again. Gingerly he took another soiled tube from the window area. This time he held it at arm's length when he filed. And then it happened again. The tube exploded and once again the shattered glass was clean.

In a glow of satisfaction, Michael addressed a letter to Dr. Paris. In firm letters, he wrote:

Dear Sir,
  The oil you noticed yesterday turned out to be liquid chlorine.

Yours faithfully,
M. Faraday.

Liquefying chlorine was a major event—a turning point in chemistry. Michael was so elated, he took the letter in person to the home of Dr. Paris in Dover Street. Handing it to the maid, he said, "Give it to him the first thing in the morning." Mission accomplished, Michael chuckled all the way home. Greeting Sarah at the door, his first words were, "I liquefied chlorine!"

At first Davy found Michael's claim hard to believe. But after further experiment he was convinced. Assured it was true, a fierce new light dominated his face. "Let's liquefy some other gases," he said.

Following this decision, the sound of explosions continued for a long time at the R.I. Fearing for his sight, Michael wore a mask as he worked. Still, he had problems. To a friend, he wrote:

I met with another explosion on Saturday evening. . . . It was from one of my tubes, and was so powerful as to drive the pieces of glass like a pistol-shot through a window. . . . My eyes were filled with glass.

By the end of these experiments, Davy had liquefied hydrogen chloride, and Michael had turned both carbon dioxide and sulfur dioxide into liquids. Neither succeeded in liquefying oxygen.°

His paper on the liquefication of chlorine completed,

°Today it is known that oxygen can be liquefied at -182° C. The result is a slightly bluish liquid.

Michael, as was his custom, turned it over to Davy for correction—or addition. With keen anticipation to see it in print, he turned his attention to other things.

That April, Phillips came sweeping into the R.I. like a hurricane. Waving the *Quarterly Journal of Science,* he demanded: "Have you read your article? I'm not sure you'll recognize all of it."

As Michael gulped the article a paragraph at a time, Phillips impatiently chewed his nails. Finally, unable to stand the pressure, he said, "Please look at the next to last paragraph—one of the two which were added by Sir Humphry."

Out loud, Michael read: "In desiring Mr. Faraday to expose the hydrate of chlorine to heat in a closed tube, it occurred to me that one of three things would happen: that it would become fluid as a hydrate; or that a decomposition of water would occur, and euchlorine and muriatic acid be formed; or that chlorine would separate in a condensed state."

As Michael read, a vacuum entered his stomach. It seemed quite obvious that Davy was making claims that were not completely true.

"Well, what do you think?" questioned Phillips, his lips compressed into the straight lines of an ax.

"All I know is that Sir Humphry did tell me to heat the hydrate in a tube; and as you can see I mentioned that in the third paragraph. Of course I don't know what was in his mind—"

"Mr. Faraday, you are very generous. Last week Sir Humphry read a paper at the Royal Society about electromagnetism. In it he inferred that you are a plagiarist. Here are his exact words—" Pulling a card from his pocket, he read:

Had not an experiment on the subject made by Dr. W. in the laboratory of the Royal Institution, and witnessed by Sir Humphry, failed merely through an accident which happened to the apparatus, he would have been the discoverer of that phenomenon.*

Michael shrugged. "I don't want to make something out of nothing," he said, a slight quiver in his voice. "All I know is that Sir Humphry is a great man."

Concerned that a mountain would be made out of this molehill, Michael shared the problem with Sarah and asked her to pray about it. Had such a tension arisen between brethren in the Sandemanian church, it would have been solved through a heart-to-heart talk and the washing of one another's feet during a service in the church.

The ultimate solution to the problem was both unique and satisfactory. While thumbing through *Nicholson's Journal,* it was learned that Northmore had succeeded in liquefying chlorine in 1805—nearly twenty years before!

Faraday was delighted that the problem was settled; and in 1824 he published an article in the *Quarterly Journal of Science* that entombed it forever. In this article on the liquefication of gases, he made it a point to give Northmore credit in being the first one to liquefy chlorine.

---

*This was not in the paper which Davy read and published. Others, however, insisted that he included these remarks even though he denied it.

15

F.R.S.

Richard Phillips approached Michael with an unusually serious look on his face. Lifting his head from some tubes he was washing, Michael was startled. "I hope you're not about to suggest an article that will ignite the Royal Institution!" he said.

"Nothing like that," laughed Phillips. "My idea is worse. Much worse."

"Ah, then I must hear it. Do I need to protect my face with a mask?"

After swiveling his head to make certain they were alone, Phillips laid a hand on Michael's shoulder. "Mr. Faraday," he said, speaking in the most serious tone Michael had ever heard him use, "I want to propose your name as a fellow in the Royal Society—"

"The Royal Society!" exclaimed Michael. "Oh, no.

No, you can't do that. I'm a Sandemanian, and we're plain people. Moreover, I'd never be elected."

"I understand how you feel, Mr. Faraday. But being able to put F.R.S. behind your name will open many a door. In the end, it will help you uncover more of God's laws—as you so aptly put it."

Michael shrugged. "If it will do that, I g-guess it will be all right. But Mr. Phillips, you'll never succeed. Never!"

"Why?"

"Because Sir Humphry is president of the Royal Society and he will never allow it. Also W—"

"Since Davy is president he's not expected to sign the proposal," replied Phillips gleefully. "Faraday, my friend, you're in!"

"One more question before you leave. Do you really think I'm worthy of such an honor?" asked Michael doubtfully.

"Of course! You've made significant breakthroughs in both electricity and chemistry. You may not know it, but you are becoming one of the top scientists of this age."

Embarrassed, Michael stared at the floor.

Curious about the Royal Society, Faraday checked out a volume on its history from the R.I. library and took it to his attic apartment. The more he studied the musty book the more impressed he became. Speaking to Sarah across the supper table, he said, "The R.S. is really old. It was founded in 1662 during the reign of Charles II. Those founders must have had a lot of courage, for their motto was *Nullius in Verba*—Don't take anyone's word for it."

"That's a good motto," interrupted Sarah. "Why would it take courage to use it?"

"Because anyone who disagreed with Aristotle in those days was accused of heresy and might be burned at the stake." Michael was silent as he buttered his bread and attacked his soup. "One of the founders was no other than the great Sir Francis Bacon, the scientist who invented inductive reasoning."

Sarah frowned. "Inductive reasoning? What's that?"

"Going from the known to the unknown. Bacon popularized experimentation." Noticing that she didn't understand, Michael laughed and patted her hand. "Sarah, you don't have to understand natural science. You're a great cook, and my closest friend. I love you as you are."

Before the end of the week, Phillips clattered up to the attic apartment two steps at a time. Glowing with success, he flung the needed certificate on the table. "Look," he all but shouted. "I already have four signatures, and the very first is that of Dr. Wollaston!"

Michael stared in unbelief. Finally, he managed a weak, "What happens next?"

"I'll get as many signatures as possible. After that, it has to be read at ten consecutive sessions of the Royal Society before it is voted on."

By the end of the month, Phillips had secured twenty-nine signatures. Waving at Michael, he boasted, "Your election is all but assured." On May 1 of that year—1823—Faraday's certificate was read at the Royal Society for the first time. While it was being read, those near Davy noticed that he began to stiffen and turn pale.

The next day as Michael was working in the laboratory, he was startled by the slamming of a door. Whirling around, he saw Davy coming toward him. Sir Humphry's face was whiter than Michael had ever seen it.

"You must take it down!" shouted the president of the R.S.

"What must I take down, sir?" inquired Michael, frowning.

"You know what I mean!" Davy spat the words with the fury of a gun spitting bullets. "I mean that dreadful certificate proposing your name as a member of the Royal Society."

"I can't take it down, Sir Humphry, for I didn't put it up. That certificate was written by others, and it was posted by others. The matter has gone too far now. I'm powerless to change a thing."

"So you refuse to take it down?"

"I'm in no position to do so, sir."

"Then I'll take it down myself. Being president of the Royal Society I have that power!" As he began to leave, his face creased with deep lines of fury and his normally calm eyes bulged like those of a person being strangled.

While Davy was stepping across the threshold of the door, Michael said, "I'm sure, Sir Humphry, that you will do that which you consider to be right for the Royal Society."

Several days after this confrontation, Phillips approached Faraday. "I think you ought to call on Warburton," he advised.

"Why Warburton?"

"Because he's a close friend of Wollaston and can swing votes."

"I thought the whirling wire affair was over," sighed Michael. "But I'll go the second mile just as you suggest."

Faraday made his call on June 5. In the interview he explained his side of the published story. Warburton listened with complete understanding. At the end of the hour-long session, he suggested that Faraday call on Wollaston. And this he did.

A few days later, Michael received a letter from Sir Humphry. Fearing what could be inside, he broke the wax seal as gingerly as if he were filing through a tube of highly compressed gas. These fears were unwarranted. It was a friendly letter which concluded, "I am, dear Faraday, very sincerely your well-wisher and friend. H. Davy."

On January 8, 1824, Michael's certificate was read at the Royal Society for the tenth time and the ballot was taken. There was only one negative vote—that of Sir Humphry Davy!

Now that he could put F.R.S. behind his name, Michael Faraday worked harder than ever. Not only did he perform countless experiments. So great was his concentration, he frequently was late to his meals or even forgot them altogether. Sometimes days would pass during which he only said a word or two to his assistant. Sarah endured this with a smile. But on one occasion when it was all she could do to keep her smile in place, Michael put down his test tube and drew her close.

While running fingers through her hair, he said, "I must tell you a story I heard about Sir Isaac Newton. It seems that when he was on the verge of proposing to his girl friend, his mind began to wander. All at once he became so absorbed in the binomial theorem for infinite quantities, he forgot he was tenderly looking into his sweetheart's eyes. In this condition, he grabbed her finger and jammed it up his pipe. He thought it was his pipe cleaner!"

"And so that's why he never married," laughed Sarah.

"That's at least one reason!" replied Michael. "Of course that may be just a story."

In April 1825, the Portable Gas Company of London sent some liquid to Faraday for analysis. The liquid was the substance left over during the manufacture of illuminating gas from whale oil.

Fascinated by the strange fluid, Faraday proceeded to chemically separate it. Eventually he isolated a new compound which he named *bicarburet of hydrogen*. He named it this because it was composed of hydrogen and carbon. Today this colorless liquid—it's not quite as heavy as water—is called benzene. At the time Faraday discovered it, the substance was a mere chemical curiosity. Forty years later, as the result of a snooze on a bus, the atomic composition of benzene was discovered. This famous discovery burst wide the doors to organic chemistry, made carbon a miracle element, and led to the development of nylon, plastics, and thousands of other things—including the fizz in soda.

Before German chemist, Kekulé von Stradonitz, dozed on the bus, he had no way of knowing that he was on the verge of a great discovery. All he knew was that he had been pondering the structure of benzene. During his forty winks he seemed to see atoms whirling in a dance. Suddenly the end of one line of atoms seized the head of another line of atoms and formed a whirling ring. Upon awakening Kekulé felt assured that he had conceived a great truth.

Unlike Archimedes who leaped out of his bath and fled naked down the streets of Syracuse shouting "Eureka! I have found it!" after his discovery of the law of specific gravity, Kekulé merely published his conception.

Kekulé's vision proved remarkably accurate. Because

of the key he provided, the industrialized world is decidedly different. In 1965—a century after the discovery—the Belgian Government issued a commemorative stamp in Kekulé's honor.

Unfortunately Faraday died before the full force of this breakthrough was understood. Nevertheless, another revolutionary breakthrough involving benzene did take place during his lifetime—and in a most unique way. This discovery changed the color of clothes and was made by a teenager. Ah, but we're getting ahead of the story![*]

Shortly after Faraday's isolation of benzene, Professor Brande called on him. "I have good news for you," he said, his blue eyes snapping in his round face. "You have been promoted. You are now Director of the Laboratory of the Royal Institution! Better yet, you were recommended to this post by no other than Sir Humphry Davy. I have a feeling, Mr. Faraday, that you understand human nature as well as you understand chemistry and electricity."

Michael chuckled. "I'm a Sandemanian. We follow the teachings of the New Testament!"

"Yes, of course." Brande coughed and looked uncomfortable. "I also have some bad news. Your salary will remain £100 a year, plus heat and candles."

"And an apartment in the attic," added Faraday, his smile even wider than before. "Don't worry about the money, Professor Brande. Material things don't mean much to Sandemanians. God looks after the sparrows and

---

[*]Seventy-five percent of the benzene produced in the United States now comes from petroleum.

166

He will take care of us. Sarah and I can manage."

"The R.I. is in a bad way financially, and things are getting worse," Brande explained. He rubbed his side-whiskers thoughtfully. "As you know, when Davy was in his prime his lectures brought in a lot of money. But now that he isn't feeling well and is away much of the time, he can no longer give them on a regular basis.

"In discussing the problem with several of my colleagues, we came to the conclusion that perhaps you could give a weekly lecture—perhaps on Friday night. We've heard you lecture before, and we think you'd be a great success."

"I'll think about it," promised Michael.

Brande started to leave and then stopped abruptly. Picking up a coil and a magnet from the table, he said, "I thought you were a chemist."

"I am. But I'm also interested in electricity. For a long time it has seemed to me that if we can convert electricity into magnetism, we ought to find a way to convert magnetism into electricity."

"I hope you succeed," replied Brande, his face masked with doubt.

16

A NEW TRAIL

During every spare moment Faraday picked up the coil and magnet and tried to conceive of a way to reach his ultimate goal of converting magnetism into electricity. But how was it to be done? Most leading scientists were certain that he was attempting the impossible.

As Faraday pondered, he considered every clue that had been uncovered. Already it was known that if lightning struck a steel pole, the pole was magnetized. Furthermore, Oersted had demonstrated with his compass and wire that flowing electricity had magnetic qualities. Having confirmed this plain truth from his own experiments, he noted in his workbook: "If it is possible to convert electricity into magnetism, then why not the converse?"

Yes, why not?

During his youth, Faraday had been deeply influenced by an article in the third edition of the *Encyclopaedia Britannica*. This article boldly suggested that instead of electricity being either one or perhaps two fluids, it might, instead, be merely vibrations. (This is the wave theory of electricity.) In time, Faraday disagreed with Newton who believed that light travels only in straight lines and that it is made up of corpuscles. Instead, he believed that light, like electricity, also consisted of vibrations. Along with Oersted who insisted that "all phenomena are produced by the same power" he tended to believe in the basic unity of all material things.

As is commonly known, water can be changed into ice and ice changed into water. This is accomplished by either lowering or increasing temperature. But Faraday's question was how to change magnetism into electricity.

In 1823, William Sturgeon, an English shoemaker who liked to experiment, wrapped eighteen turns of *bare* copper wire around a U-shaped iron and ran a current through the wire.° While the current was flowing, the iron became a magnet. Astonished, Sturgeon named the new devise *electromagnet*. He soon proved that his electromagnet could lift twenty times as much iron as its own weight. Also, he discovered that the moment the current was turned off, the magnetism stopped. This discovery eventually had enormous consequences.

Faraday was fascinated with electromagnets. Still, they did not produce electricity!

Wondering if it was possible to cause current to go from one wire to another without being physically connected, Faraday began to experiment. His diary tells us

---

° Insulated wire was unknown at this time.

what he did in November. "Two copper wires were tied close together, a thickness of paper only intervening for a length of five feet." One of the wires made a circuit to the battery; and the other was connected to a galvanometer to detect any current, should it flow. The battery had forty plates.

As Faraday gingerly completed the contact with the galvanometer, he breathlessly watched the needle. The tiniest flicker would indicate that he was on the razor's edge of a major discovery. The needle, however, showed no response. After making certain the connections to the battery were secure, he connected the galvanometer again. It was still as dead as a nail in a coffin.

Having failed with the wires parallel, he now tried several other positions—including the winding of one wire into a coil and the thrusting of the other wire through its axis. In each experiment the needle remained stationary.° Discouraged at the end of this unsuccessful day—it was November 25, 1825—Faraday fumbled for his diary. After he had described what he had done, he wrote: "No results." But before closing the book, he added. "The galvanometer was not a very delicate one."

Sometime during this general period an amazing experiment was performed by Francois Arago in France. Hanging a magnetized needle over a copper disc, he found that when the disc was rotated the needle also rotated. A similar experiment was performed in England by S. H. Christie and Peter Barlow with similar results. But since their disc was made of iron which could be magnetized, their experiment was not as impressive as that of Arago.

° Had he connected the battery last, the needle would have flicked!

The story of the nonmagnetic copper disc caused a sensation. What did it mean? Scientists all over the world tried to ferret out a satisfactory answer.

During these years, Faraday had other things to do in addition to trying to convert magnetism into electricity. For one thing, in order to keep the Royal Institution solvent, he had agreed to give a lecture each Friday night. Since Davy was no longer giving them, and the others who tried to fill his place were unspeakably dull, Faraday determined to be at his best. As he considered how to accomplish this, he remembered the way Edward Magrath had helped him with his English years before. He now approached him and requested help.

"Yes, I'll come each week the day after the lecture and suggest improvements," promised his friend.

The lectures started in the laboratory. But within weeks Faraday was forced to move to the R.I. auditorium where as a youth he had listened spellbound to Sir Humphry Davy. Standing in the same place where the great Sir Humphry had stood was an emotional experience. As he viewed the place over the clock where he had sat in the gallery, a lump formed in his throat. At that time, he had dreamed of being the assistant. Now he was the lecturer! It was unbelievable. In almost no time each lecture was packed to the four walls and the money flowed in.

During 1827 a flattering offer came. "We would like you to be Professor of Chemistry at the University of London," said the spokesman.

Michael's eyes glistened. But he refused even to consider the offer. He replied firmly, "The Royal Institution has been a source of pleasure and knowledge to me.

I remember the privileges and protection it has afforded me during past years."

Two years later, Faraday was asked to lecture at the Royal Academy at Woolwich. "You will only have to give twenty lectures a year, and your annual pay will be £200," said the official who had contacted him.

Since this work did not interfere with his duties at the R.I., and since his salary was still only £100 a year, he accepted. Sarah was an expert penny pincher. Nevertheless, there were plenty of places for the extra money. For one thing, he still supported his mother.

During these turbulent years, Faraday was saddened by the fact that Sir Humphry was losing his health. He finally died on May 29, 1829, in Geneva where he had fled seeking a remedy. Before he passed away, he was questioned about his greatest discoveries and inventions. The list was a long one. It included at least four elements—there is an argument about his study of iodine—and the Davy Safety Lamp.

As the visitor turned to leave, Sir Humphry motioned him closer. Drumming his nails on the book he was reading, Davy said, "My greatest discovery was Michael Faraday!"

Busy writing books, giving lectures, and performing experiments, Faraday's years seemed to flash by with the brilliance and speed of a comet. Converting magnetism into electricity remained uppermost in his mind. Again and again he tried. But each time he had to conclude wearily in his diary, "No results."

Early in his marriage, Michael had developed the habit of going for long walks with Sarah. His favorite time was when the sun was disappearing over the horizon. The big ball of fire reminded him of the time he had proposed and was accepted at Dover. It also brought to his mind the greatness of his Creator. Often as he studied the sun he got new ideas for experiments.

The Bible and the church also remained uppermost in his life. He liked to underline passages in his Bible. A heavily marked and favorite one was Job 9:20, "If I justify myself, mine own mouth shall condemn me: if I say, I am perfect, it shall also prove me perverse."

The Faradays seldom missed services in the Sandemanian meetinghouse. Being an elder, Michael often preached. When the elders refused to serve the Lord's Supper on a certain Sunday because of disharmony in the flock, he was brokenhearted—especially since his own wife was part of the disagreement. He took great satisfaction in his membership in the Royal Society and signed all of his publications with F.R.S. after his name. But he was much more concerned about his Christianity than his membership in the R.S. even though many of the great, including Sir Isaac Newton, Sir Francis Bacon, Robert Boyle, and Benjamin Franklin had been members.

To Faraday, the meetinghouse in St. Paul's Alley was a place of worship, inspiration, fellowship. In addition, he loved the singing and preaching. True, many of the sermons were preached by semiliterate elders. But their double negatives and mispronounced words didn't bother Faraday. He drank from the same fountain from which they drank, and so why should it matter if some said *ax* for ask or if Cockney-fashion they dropped their h's?

With them, Faraday believed the words of Jesus: "Ask, and it shall be given you; seek, and ye shall find; knock, and it shall be opened unto you: for every one that asketh receiveth; and he that seeketh findeth; and to him that knocketh it shall be opened" (Matthew 7:7, 8).

As for himself, he did a lot of seeking, knocking—and receiving!

Faraday's life was not all research and worship. He loved children. Frequently when they came for a visit, he showed them simple experiments, made them candy and toys, and sometimes amused everyone by scooting through the aisles of the R.I. on a self-made velocipede.

Each Friday night Faraday seemed to put more zest in his lecture than he had the week before. Many of his talks at this time were on electricity and magnetism. Perhaps he hoped that like Oersted he would accidentally make a discovery in the midst of a lecture. His lectures were all up to date. As soon as new ideas were published, he included them in a lecture and explained them according to his own theories.

Usually the entire audience was spellbound as he spoke and conducted demonstrations with his apparatus. Nevertheless, on one occasion a certain Mr. Fuller, who was sitting in a front seat, went to sleep and began to snore loudly!

Disturbed, Faraday stopped and looked. Following a painful silence, a man near Fuller began to clap. At this point Fuller awakened, joined in the clapping, and in his deep, sonorous voice, shouted, "Bravo!" This twist of events so convulsed the crowd it was a long time before Faraday could quiet them and continue with his lecture.

In 1829 an American experimenter, Joseph Henry, heard, about Sturgeon's electromagnet. Like Faraday, he had had little formal schooling and was completely intrigued with electricity. In his youth, while apprenticed to a watchmaker, he made a trip into the country. While there, he chased a rabbit. The rabbit leaped inside an empty church and disappeared through a missing plank in the floor. Having lost the rabbit, Henry looked around for something to occupy his mind. Fortunately, he found a book on natural history. This book inspired him to become a scientist.

Noting that Sturgeon had wrapped the U-shaped iron with *bare* wire, Henry wrapped his iron bar with wire which he had insulated by wrapping it in silk. His results were amazing. At a demonstration at Princeton, Henry's electromagnet lifted 750 pounds of iron. And later he lifted no less than a ton at Yale. The professors were goggle-eyed as they watched.

Late in August 1831, Faraday was suddenly gripped with a fascinating new idea. Indeed, he was so intrigued he went to his apartment at an unexpected hour. "Sarah," he said, his voice quivering with excitement, "do you have an old calico apron?"

"I-I think so." She looked at him curiously. Had overwork affected his brain? "The next time I clean I'll keep my eyes open for it—"

"Oh, but I want it now. Immediately!"

"Can't you wait until this evening?"

"I'm afraid not. The need is urgent."

A few minutes later Sarah handed him a threadbare apron and Faraday descended to his laboratory two steps at a time.

17

BREAKTHROUGH

With more than usual care, Michael ripped his wife's calico apron into narrow strips. Next, he carefully wrapped the strips around the bare copper wire. Having completely insulated it he proceeded to the next step.

Faraday's diary for August 29, 1831, tells us exactly what he did:

> Have had an iron ring made (soft iron), iron round and ⅞ inches thick and ring 6 inches in external diameter. Wound many coils of copper wire round one half, the coils being separated by twine and calico—there were 3 lengths of wire about 24 feet long and they could be connected as one length or used as separate lengths."

As he surveyed the ring, he made certain that the length of wire on one side was not connected to the wire on the other side. Assured of this, he connected one side to his galvanometer. Then he took the ends of the wire on the other side and carefully connected one end to the battery. With this wire securely in place, he touched its other end to the battery. As he did this, his eyes were fixed on the galvanometer. At the exact moment of contact, the needle twitched and Faraday's eyes jumped. But after the twitch, the needle settled back to its original position.

His heart jumping, Faraday examined all of the contacts to see why the needle had gone down. Yes, the contacts were secure. Yes, the current was still flowing. Why, then, was there no action? As he puzzled over this problem, he disconnected a wire to the battery. After all, there was no value in wasting electricity. And then it happened again. The needle twitched. Only this time it twitched in the opposite direction!

To make certain his eyes weren't deceiving him, Faraday made and broke the contact several times. No, he hadn't been deceived! Each time the connection was made or broken the needle twitched.° Thoroughly excited, he addressed a letter to Phillips who happened to be away from London. "I am busy now with Electromagnetism," he wrote, "and I think I have got hold of a good thing, but can't say: it may be a weed instead of a fish."

Faraday now tried to figure out what had happened. Because he had used a battery, he obviously had not

---

°At the time Faraday did not realize it, but he had just discovered the principle of the transformer. The reason the needle only flicked when the contact was either made or broken was because he was dealing with *direct current*. This is the major reason our homes are powered with *alternating* current.

generated electricity. Still, he had created an electromagnet just as Henry had done; and, in addition, he had transferred current from one wire to another. Had this been done by magnetism? He didn't know, but he was determined to find out.

Following several other experiments which varied only in detail with the one with the iron ring, Faraday wrapped coils around a block of wood instead of iron to see what would happen. Again the needle twitched just as it had twitched before; but this time the movement was not as pronounced. Still, current had flowed from wire to wire without any physical connection. This flow, he strongly suspected, was because of magnetism.

He now reasoned that if electricity could be made to flow by electromagnetism, it should also be made to flow through the use of an ordinary bar magnet. Nevertheless, the problem remained: how was this to be done?

By October 17, 1831, he had several definite ideas he wanted to try. From his notes, written on that date, we learn that he wrapped a paper cylinder with

> 8 helices [coils] of copper wire going in the same direction. . . . The 8 ends of the helices at one end of the cylinder were cleaned and fastened together as a bundle. So were the 8 other ends. These compound ends were then connected with the Galvanometer by long copper wires—then a cylindrical bar magnet ¾ inch in diameter and 8½ inch in length . . . [was] inserted into the end of the cylinder.

Faraday's face fell as he eagerly watched the needle. There was not the slightest twitch. Instead, it was as dead as a discarded fishhook. Discouraged, he jerked the magnet from the coil. That jerk changed the history of electricity!

Fortunately for science, just as Faraday jerked the magnet he also glanced at the meter and noticed that it twitched. Breathlessly, he pushed the magnet in again and then pulled it out. This caused the needle to twitch when it went in and also to twitch when he pulled it out. All at once Faraday realized he had succeeded in his quest. Beside himself with joy, he leaped up and down and danced around the room while he shouted, "It works! It works! It works! I've changed magnetism into electricity."*

After he had calmed down, he pushed the magnet through the whole length of the coil and pulled it out on the opposite side. He now discovered that when the magnet went in, the needle was deflected in one direction; and when it was pulled out from the opposite side, the needle was deflected in the opposite direction.

Faraday's next problem was to develop apparatus that would create a flow of electricity that would continue to move in the same direction. Hot on the trail of this next advance, he remembered Arago's copper disc.

Eventually, he arranged for a copper disc to be rotated between the poles of permanent magnets. He then connected one wire of the galvanometer to the axle of the disc and the other to a sliding contact on the edge.

Yes, it worked. When the disc was rotated, the needle moved in one direction and remained in that position as long as the disc was whirled. True, there wasn't very much current; nevertheless there was current, and this is what mattered.

---

*In America Joseph Henry, unknown to Faraday, was performing similar experiments. Likewise, he succeeded. Faraday, however, got the credit for inventing the dynamo because he was the first to publish the story.

Michael Faraday had invented the dynamo!

Did Michael Faraday know that his discovery would revolutionize the world? Probably not. At least he did not envision the gigantic powerhouses of our time. However, he knew the dynamo had value. Shortly after he had invented it, Prime Minister Sir Robert Peel came to the R.I. laboratory to witness a demonstration. After viewing it from all angles and seeing the spark it produced, he asked, "What good is it?"

"I know not," replied Faraday with a chuckle, "but I'll wager that one day your government will tax it!"

Faraday's worldwide recognition began to rocket. The Royal Society conferred on him the Copley Medal—their highest award. Other countries, also, recognized his achievements. Indeed, by the time of his death he had received nearly one hundred medals, honors, or diplomas.

In 1832 a letter came to him from Oxford University. Opening it in the presence of his wife, he learned that the university had voted him a Doctor of Civil Law degree. "I-I can hardly believe it," he said, sinking limply into a chair.

"Will I now have to call you Dr. Faraday?" asked Sarah.

"Certainly not. But you know the greatest part of the honor is not the degree. The greatest part is that John Dalton will be receiving a D.C.L. the same day. In my opinion, Dalton has made the greatest contributions to the understanding of matter of anyone in our age. His atomic theory is now the basis of all chemistry."

Suddenly Michael began to laugh. "Dalton may have a problem when he gets his degree. As you know, he's a Quaker—"

"So?"

"Quakers are supposed to avoid loud colors, and the robes we'll be required to wear are bright red—"

"So what will he do?"

"He's color blind and won't know the difference!"

Michael's guess was correct. Even though Dalton's robe was as red as a cat's tongue, no one was unkind enough to tell him. Indeed, he was so convinced it was a drab Quaker color, he boldly wore it into a Quaker meetinghouse!

Two years later, Faraday had additional reason to smile with and at his friend, the father of the atomic theory. At that time it was arranged for Dalton to be presented to His Majesty, King William IV at St. James' Palace. But how was this to be done according to strict protocol? There were two difficulties: those presented to the king were required to wear a sword. Also it was essential to enter the king's chamber with one's head uncovered.

Quakers being pacifists, Dalton refused to wear a sword; and because Quakers refused to doff their hats to anyone, there was a hat problem. A protocol genius, however, masterminded the situation to the satisfaction of everyone. Dalton was asked to wear his Oxford robe. This robe served to hide the fact that the sixty-eight-year-old man was swordless. The hat problem, however, was more difficult.

In the end, this difficulty was solved by telling Dalton that the velvet cap "was a mark of office rather than a covering for the head." Dalton thus went into the chamber bareheaded.

Some of Dalton's friends had secretly tried to arrange for him to be knighted. When he heard of this, he quickly put an end to their hopes by saying, "I will not bow my knee to anyone on earth!"

Now that Dr. Faraday was a world celebrity, all kinds of extra work came his way. "Would you analyze this for us?" asked a leading manufacturer. "What do you recommend for this operation?" inquired another. With these requests came money. In 1830 he earned £1000 on the side. And now he was in a position to earn much more. But Faraday was a Sandemanian. He just wasn't interested in money or what money could buy. In 1832 he wrote to Richard Phillips: "I'll have to cut down. These commercial investigations interfere with my thinking, with my own research."

Faraday was concerned about further advances in electricity. Also he was wondering if he could bend light with magnetism. In addition, he needed time to write books about his experiments and discoveries. Since in his lifetime he performed more than 5,000 experiments, this was a time-consuming task.

Refusing outside work gradually cut down his income. By 1832 his outside income had dropped to £155; and six years later he had no extra income at all. This lack of money did not bother either Michael or Sarah. Her only interest was to keep Michael going, and his only interest was to continue finding and publishing more of God's secrets.

In 1833 the British Government granted an annual pension of £150 to John Dalton. When Faraday heard about it, he rejoiced. It was about time someone rewarded the old man for his endless work! As for himself, he was quite happy with what he was earning even though it was still only £100 a year, plus heat and candles—and the attic apartment. And then an unusual letter came to him from Sir James South, a Fellow of the Royal Society.

Having read the letter by candlelight in the apartment, Michael exclaimed, "Look, Sarah, Sir James has written that application has been made to Prime Minister Peel to grant us a pension of £300 a year!"

After reading the letter herself, Sarah laughingly asked, "And what are you going to do about it, Dr. Faraday?"

Michael thrust up his hands in dismay. "I'm going to refuse it, of course. There's no reason I should receive money I haven't earned. After all, we have plenty to eat, a laboratory in which to work, a wonderful church to attend, and besides all of that we have access to God's universe."

That was the end of their conversation about the pension that night. The rest of the evening was spent in reading and enjoying the fine soup Sarah had prepared. "You are the best cook in the world," said Michael drawing her close.

The next day Faraday wrote a letter to Sir James in which he told him that he would not accept a pension even if it were offered.

Several days later, Sarah's father cornered Michael. "Prime Minister Peel believes no one deserves a government pension as much as you do," he said, speaking in low, confidential tones.

"Mr. Barnard, I've already turned it down," shrugged Michael.

"I think you've made a mistake. No one has earned a pension more than you. Your discoveries have increased the wealth of England. Besides, what will Sarah do after the Lord has summoned you home?"

Faraday hung his head. "I-I never thought of it in those terms," he admitted sheepishly.

By the time it was officially known that Michael Faraday would accept a pension after all, Sir Robert Peel had been replaced by Lord Melbourne. In due course Michael received a note summoning him to an interview with the prime minister. No one knows precisely what was said during this interview. It is known, however, that Melbourne had unkind things to say about scientists, authors, and others who sought financial relief from government. Also it is known that he used the word *humbug* and several others similar to it.

Annoyed, Faraday politely excused himself in the midst of the conversation. That evening he left his card and a letter at the home of the prime minister. The letter stated that he had no interest whatsoever in the proposed pension.

A lady who happened to be a close friend of both Faraday and Melbourne tried to adjust the matter—to become a go-between. But Faraday was stubborn. He had made up his mind and even refused to see the P.M. again.

"You deserve the pension," she insisted, nodding her head.

"The word humbug is a harsh word. I'm not a humbug. Sarah and I can get along without a pension. I can get extra work if I need it."

"Yes, but that extra work will keep you from important experiments."

Faraday hesitated.

Seeing that she had scored a point, she asked, "Mr. Faraday what would the prime minister have to do in order for you to accept a pension?"

After considerable thought, Faraday stated his terms: "I should require from his lordship what I have no right or reason to expect—that he would grant a written apology for the words he permitted himself to use to me."

Since the affair had gotten into the press, Lord Melbourne found himself in an embarrassing situation. This was especially so because Faraday had become a national hero. A written apology was the easy way out, and so he wrote one and mailed it to Faraday. It was full and frank and to the point.

Satisfied, Michael Faraday accepted the £300 pension!

18

HONORS

Not everyone in England appreciated Michael Faraday and what he was doing. To many, the ability to change magnetism into electricity was a dangerous step backwards.

At a fair in Oxford, someone approached Faraday and asked him to demonstrate his newly invented dynamo. Viewing the fat spark it produced, a dean from the university scowled.

"I am sorry, sir," he commented, walking away and shaking his head. "Yes, I am sorry you invented such a thing." Stopping in the middle of the room, he repeated his former statement with additional emphasis. At the door, he paused with a hand on the knob. This time with even more emphasis, he said, "*Indeed*, I am sorry for it. It is putting new arms into the hands of the incendiary!"

The dean may have been inspired to make this statement because at the time a lot of damage had been done by a gang of firebugs and the stories were dominating the papers. Unfortunately the distinguished man's words were misunderstood by a reporter. The Oxford papers quoted him as having said, "It is putting new arms into the hands of the *infidel.*"

More than most, Michael Faraday was convinced the world was entering a startling new era. The candles of his boyhood were rapidly being replaced by gas lamps. By 1833, London alone had 40,000 of these sputtering affairs. Only five when Edward Jenner used cowpox to develop a vaccine against smallpox, Michael remembered his elders fussing over it. Some were certain that those vaccinated would either grow horns or moo like a cow!

By 1803 the Royal Family had broken much of this prejudice by submitting to vaccination. The Germans made it compulsory. Indeed, even the backward Russians had started to use vaccine. They celebrated this event by naming the first Russian girl to be vaccinated, Vaccinov! The War of 1812 with the United States was now over, and so were the Napoleonic Wars. To celebrate the latter fact, Waterloo Bridge was completed on June 18, 1817— the second anniversary of the French defeat.

Even after Faraday's breakthroughs in changing magnetism into electricity, electrical science was merely an infant in a cradle. Still, he had faith that someday this mysterious force would serve a useful purpose. His compulsion to prepare the masses for what was ahead grew as the years slipped by. Taking advantage of his opportunities to explain new discoveries to his audience on Friday night, he worked harder than ever on his lectures.

Revealing scientific law was to him just as important as the preaching of a sermon. Moreover, he obeyed spiritual laws with the same assurance with which he obeyed scientific laws. Because of this, he was always quick to forgive.

Remembering how as a youth he had been moved by Davy's lectures at the Royal Institute, Faraday conceived the idea of annually presenting such a series aimed at juveniles. In early years while he was unusually busy in the laboratory, he often skipped a year or two between each series. After 1840, his lectures became a celebrated annual event and the tickets were in wide demand.

The most popular of these juvenile series was entitled, "The Chemical History of a Candle." Because of its popularity, this series was often repeated.

With apparatus in hand, Faraday illustrated his lectures from beginning to end. With great skill he kept the children on the edges of their seats. "But how does the flame get hold of the fuel?" he asked, his face a question mark.

Pausing just right for maximum effect, and holding the candle for all to see, he answered, "It is by what is called capillary attraction that the fuel is conveyed to the part where combustion goes on, and is deposited there, not in a careless way, but very beautifully in the very midst of the center of action, which takes place around it."

Aware that capillary attraction might be hard for some to understand, he was prepared to explain it.

"Now I am going to give you one or two instances of capillary attraction. It is that kind of action or attraction which makes two things that do not dissolve in each other still hold together. When you wash your hands, you wet them thoroughly. You take a little soap to make the adhesion better, and you find your hands remain wet. This is the kind of attraction of which I am about to speak. And what's more, if your hands are not soiled—if you put your finger into a little warm water, the water will creep a little way up your finger, though you may not stop to examine it.

"I have here a substance which is rather porous—a column of salt—and I will pour into the plate at the bottom, not water, as it appears, but a saturated solution of salt which cannot absorb more, so that the action which you will see will not be due to its dissolving anything. We may consider the plate to be the candle, and the salt the wick, and this solution the melted tallow. (I have colored the fluid, so that you may see the action better.)

"Observe now that as I pour the salt into the solution, it rises and gradually creeps up the salt higher and higher. Provided the column does not tumble over, it will go to the top."

With such simple illustrations, Faraday gave a rudimentary outline of some of the most difficult phenomena. Likewise, he inspired everyone to love simple things.

To Faraday a simple candle was one of the most beautiful things in existence. "In each candle," he declared, "you have the glittering beauty of gold and silver, and the still higher luster of jewels like the ruby and diamond. But none of these rival the brilliancy and beauty of a flame. What diamond can shine like a flame? It owes its luster at nighttime to the very flame shining upon it. The flames shines in darkness, but the light which the diamond has is as nothing until the flame shines upon it, when it is brilliant again."

His lectures explained the reason for the shape and

brilliance of the candle, the reason the entire candle does not burn at once, the secret of combustion, and more.

All classes of society crowded Faraday's lectures. Among his distinguished guests were Queen Victoria's husband, the Prince Consort, and their eldest son, the Prince of Wales, later to become King Edward VII. The fact that royalty attended his lectures was headlined in the newspapers and enabled Faraday to spread his ideas and the use of the new discoveries even more effectively.

Perhaps Faraday's greatest lecture success came at a time when he was unaware of it. In 1852 a fourteen-year-old by the name of William Henry Perkin took a seat in the gallery of the Royal Institution. The exact seat is unknown. Still it is quite likely that he sat near the clock—the place selected by Michael Faraday when he used the four tickets given him by Mr. Dance to hear Sir Humphry.

Faraday's lectures at this time were on electricity. Perkin attended several. Faraday's charm and the facts he demonstrated gripped him like a tightened vice. The sparks from the dynamo, and the rotating wire, almost pulled him off his seat. Even more than before, the young teenager—who always came in a high-collared shirt and black bow tie—determined to be a scientist.

During his eighteenth year, a mere four years later, Perkin's employer, A. W. von Hofmann, mumbled out loud that it would be great if quinine could be manufactured out of coal tar. If this could be done, it would save Europe the expense of importing this cure for malaria from South America.

Perkin snapped at the suggestion. Ever since Kekulé had drawn a diagram of the atomic structure of a molecule of Faraday's benzene, chemists had been juggling various atomic combinations as they attempted to create new products. During an experiment in which Perkin mixed potassium dichromate with aniline—a coal tar chemical—he suddenly noticed a purplish glint at the base of his beaker. Curious as to what it might be, he tried to dissolve it with alcohol. The response was immediate. The alcohol became a high-quality purple.

By accident, Perkin had discovered the first synthetic dye!

This was a monumental discovery, for until then the world had to be content with dyes made from vegetables, animals, or insects. For centuries purple dye had been produced from shell fish, and red dye from the female *coccus cacti*—an insect that thrives on cactus plants in Mexico.

With the cooperation of his father and elder brother, Perkin went into business. The business prospered and by the time he was twenty-three he was the world authority on dyes. At that age he was summoned to lecture before the London Chemical Society. Sitting in his audience was Michael Faraday. This was one of the highlights of Faraday's life. It was a proof that his lectures had been effective and that their influence would spread to future generations.

Year after year his candle lectures gained in popularity. In time, six of the lectures were taken down in shorthand and published in a 223-page book entitled *The Chemical History of a Candle*. The book became extremely popular and was translated into many languages.

One afternoon an expensive coach stopped at the Royal Institution and a footman clothed in immaculate livery called on Faraday. Snapping to attention, he said,

191

"I have a letter for Dr. Michael Faraday from Her Majesty the Queen."

The letter was an invitation to have lunch with Queen Victoria the next Sunday!

"What will I do?" inquired Faraday, hugging Sarah.

"Oh, I'm so proud!" she said.

"Yes, but Sunday is the day we go to church. What will the elders think?"

Sarah stomped her foot. "It doesn't matter what they think," she replied, her blue eyes bright with a determined light.

"I agree with you. Still, Elder B. and Elder W. are in charge this month. They could take away my eldership!"

"True. But I think you should go. And please give my regards to Her Majesty."

Although fearing what might happen, Michael Faraday had lunch with Queen Victoria. It was a great occasion and Michael repeated all the details he could remember to Sarah. "Did you ever dream that I would have such an honor?" he asked when he was finished.

"Of course," she said, as she moved onto his lap and ran fingers through his whitening hair. "I've never understood Newton's laws or Dalton's atomic theories. Nevertheless, I've always loved you, and I've always known that your greatest desire was to stay in harmony with the Creator. And Michael, that's what counts!"

Within two weeks, the Sandemanian elders called on Faraday. "We don't want to do you no harm," said Elder B. "But you know us Sandemanians believe in the complete separation of church and state. Not only have you reflected on us, but you did it on Sunday. Brother Faraday, if you'll publicly repent we will forget the matter. Otherwise—"

"Otherwise, what?" asked Faraday, tears in his eyes.

"Otherwise, you will forfeit your eldership."

"I don't want that to happen. I love the brethren—"

"Brother Faraday, there jist ain't no other way," said the spokesman.

Since Michael Farday refused to repent, he was duly suspended as an elder. The Faradays were brokenhearted over the matter. His face damp from tears, he expressed his grief to Sarah. "My parents attended here from the time they moved to London, and you and I have attended here all our lives. Sarah, it's all I can do to keep from being angry. But I refuse to be angry. Anger would be beneath me!"

In spite of this action, the Faradays continued to attend the Sandemanian meetinghouse in St. Paul's Alley. Even so, the problem continued to gnaw at their hearts.

After a time of prayer, Bible reading, and fasting, Michael Faraday made up his mind on how he would respond to the situation. But as always—when it concerned spiritual matters—he kept his intentions to himself.

The following Sunday as he approached their place of worship. Faraday did so with a light heart. His only worry was that Elder B. and Elder W. might not be there. As usual, the slum area containing the meetinghouse was littered with drunks. Some were lying in their own vomit. Others were sprawled on the steps of the rickety tenement houses. As always, the broken windows were stuffed with filthy rags and the webs of clotheslines snaked in all directions, while the patched garments they supported shuddered in the breeze.

St. Paul's Alley was like one of Hogarth's more dramatic prints. It never changed.

After the sermon, the congregation separated. The women filed into one room and the men into another. Faraday followed the men and drew the door shut. After each had removed his shoes and stockings, an elder read the story of how Jesus had washed His disciples' feet in the Upper Room as recorded in the Gospel of John. Having closed the Bible, the group, keeping their voices low, joined in singing a hymn. Then Michael Faraday wrapped the end of a long towel around his waist and knelt in front of Elder B., the spokesman who had said that if he didn't repent he would lose his eldership.

After washing and drying the man's feet, Faraday exchanged places with him and Elder B. washed his feet. Finished, the two stood and embraced one another. The other men in the room did likewise. At the conclusion of this oft-repeated service, the men and women reassembled and shared the Lord's Supper.

In subsequent months, Michael Faraday was reinstated as an elder and, as before, preached when it was his turn. His religious faith was deep—and profound. He was just as certain that he and the congregation were a part of the mystical body of Christ as he was of the laws of gravity. In his excellent biography on Faraday, L. Pearce Williams commented:

> His true humility lay in a profound consciousness of his debt to his Creator. That Michael Faraday, poor, uneducated son of a journeyman blacksmith and a country maid was permitted to glimpse the beauty of the eternal laws of nature was a never-ending source of wonder to him.

Now that his spiritual position in the congregation was restored, Faraday felt free to devote himself to even more experiments in the coming years.

19

SUNSET

Having accidentally shattered a test tube, Faraday shuffled to the door to summon the janitor—an Irishman who had been with the R.I. for the previous six months. But even though the slender moustached man was standing in the aisle with a broom in his fist, Faraday could not remember his name.

His poor memory was slowly getting worse. At the end of an hour's rest in the apartment, he felt slightly better. "My mind has become a sieve," he complained. "I can remember the past. Davy is as real as ever. It's the present that's gone."

Before retiring that night he had such an acute dizzy spell he almost stumbled over a chair. "You must see a doctor!" exclaimed Sarah, rushing to his aid. After thorough examination the physician said, "You've been working much too hard. Cut your hours in half and—and give up your Friday night lectures. I've heard many of them and they require far too much work."

"I'll ease up in the lab," promised Faraday reluctantly. "But I can't give up my lectures. The R.I. needs the income! Besides, I enjoy them. Giving them up would be like giving up my right arm."

"If you can't give them up, don't put so much work into them."

The doctor looked grim.

Working half time for several months seemed to help; but as Faraday's health improved so did the length of his working hours. An idea for an experiment would possess him, sometimes early in the morning, and then he could hardly wait until daylight to begin work in the laboratory.

This was an exciting period. On May 6, 1840, Britain issued the world's first postage stamp. Faraday smiled grimly. "Now the people will have to pay the postage before they mail me their letters. This will save us a lot of money and we won't have to keep loose change around!" he said, smiling broadly. (Until then, the person who received the letter had to pay the postage.)

Many were skeptical of this revolutionary idea and declared that it could never work. But it did. Indeed, the United States began to issue postage stamps seven years later!

From boyhood, Faraday had dreamed of the time when messages could be transmitted instantaneously from one point to another. Across the years, he had watched the development of the electromagnet. Then he learned that on May 24, 1844, Samuel F. B. Morse had sent a telegram from Washington to Baltimore. The historic message was, "What hath God wrought?" Faraday was delighted with this success—and the message. Like Newton, Morse had stood on the shoulders of others—especially those of Joseph Henry—and had invented something that would benefit the world.

Again, overwork laid Faraday low. "You must stop straining your mind," said Sarah. "You work all day in the lab, you think at the table when your mind should be at ease, and even when you're supposed to be asleep your mind is working on ideas. You've already accomplished more than a dozen men."

But Michael Faraday refused to stop working. For years he had been turning the pages in the book of God's laws and each new page seemed more interesting than the previous one.

Desperate, Sarah announced that she and her brother George were going to Switzerland for a long rest—and that he was to go with them. To give Faraday's mind a rest, the doctors ordered that he could not take any scientific journals with him. "Your fertile mind must be at ease," they said.

During the nine months in Switzerland, Faraday stayed away from scientific journals and research. He could not, however, refrain from keeping a journal. He was intrigued at the way the Swiss made nails by hand. On August 2, 1841, he wrote: "Clout nailmaking goes on here . . . and is a very neat and pretty operation to observe. I love a smith's shop and anything related to smithery. *My father was a smith.*"

At Interlaken he especially enjoyed the sunsets on the crisp mountain peaks. He had no scientific papers to read, but those sunsets spoke to him in the same way as the books of Newton and Galileo. For a long time he had believed "that the various forms under which the forces of matter are made manifest have one common origin. This strong persuasion," he added, "extends to the powers of light."

Also believing that one force can be changed into another, as electricity can be changed into magnetism and magnetism into electricity, he wondered if he could show that magnetism could effect light. It was a daring thought!

Back in London, Faraday remained in forced semi-retirement. By 1845 he was much better. Again his gray eyes sparkled and his old humor returned. He had gained a second wind. Late in August of that year he began to experiment with magnetism and light. As before, he collided with one stonewall after another stonewall and had to conclude his records with the dismal words, "No result."

It was disheartening. Still, he gritted his teeth and continued. He felt confident that in the end he would succeed.

Time after time he focused polarized light (light that has been filtered so that it vibrates in only one direction)° through a square of glass and tried to affect its passage with magnetism. At last, by use of some glass he had made in 1830, he succeeded. Exalted by this breakthrough, he wrote, "When contrary magnetic poles were on the same side, *there was an effect produced on the polarized ray, and thus magnetic force and light were proved to have relation to each other.*"

Knowing that only a few would understand the signifi-

° Photographers use polarizing filters in order to avoid glare when, for example, they are photographing objects through a glass window.

cance of this discovery, he added prophetically: "This fact will most likely prove exceedingly fertile and of great value in the investigation of both conditions of natural force." (He was referring to light and magnetism.) This was probably the understatement of his life, as we shall see in the epilogue.

Even though peaking with new fame in scientific circles, Michael Faraday refused to take time from outside experiments to earn extra income.

Happy years of routine stretched ahead for the Faradays. But 1846 proved to be an unhappy one, for in August of that year Faraday's brother Robert was killed in a driving accident. The two had been very close and Michael had never forgotten that it was Robert who had paid his way to the Tatum lectures.

Immediately after the resignation of Lord Wrottlesly as president of the Royal Society a committee of distinguished men called on Faraday. "We want you to become the new president of the Royal Society," they announced.

"That's an extremely high honor!" exclaimed Faraday, thoroughly shocked.

"Will you accept the honor?" they pressed.

"I'll talk it over with my wife and let you know in the morning."

"Well, what's your decision?" they asked the next day.

"I'm flattered," he replied. "However, I must remain plain Michael Faraday until the last."

Following the death of the Duke of Northumberland, Faraday was asked to take his place as president of the Royal Institution. "It would be a fitting climax to your nearly half a century with us," said the leader of the committee.

Again Michael refused. "The responsibilities would cut into the time I spend on research," he explained.

Wires, chemicals, test tubes, microscopes, batteries, and dynamos were more important to Faraday than honors and money. While busy with an experiment, Michael was approached by an employee of the Royal Mint.

Noticing Faraday's shuffling gait, bent shoulders, and snowy hair, the employee inquired, "Have you been here for a long time?"

"Nearly half a century," replied Faraday with a smile.

"Are you the janitor?"

Faraday shrugged. "In a way."

"Do they pay you well?"

"They could do a little better, I think." By this time Michael's smile had spread until gaps in his teeth caused by recent extractions could be seen.

"Maybe I can make a helpful suggestion to management," said the employee kindly. Lifting a pencil, he asked, "What is your name, sir?"

"Michael Faraday!" replied the Sandemanian elder, returning to his experiments.

Across the years, climbing the steps to their two-room apartment in the attic of the Royal Institution had become a tiresome chore for the Faradays—and especially to Sarah. Sarah had become slightly lame and the many steps had become a burden.

Learning about this problem, Queen Victoria offered them a rent-free house near Hampton Court. It was a lovely house in a distinguished neighborhood. But Michael shook his head. "We don't have the funds for the necessary repairs," he explained.

Refusing to give up, the Queen paid for all the

200

necessary renovations—and had them done in such a way the Faradays would not have to climb steps. Profoundly thankful, Michael and Sarah moved in.

After 1862 Michael's health began a rapid decline. The even-flamed candle of his life began to sputter. On June 20 of that year he completed preparation for what was to be his final Friday night lecture. At the end of his notes, he indicated reasons for terminating this part of his work. Among other things, he listed: *Loss of memory. . . . Inability to draw. . . . Dimness and forgetfulness. . . .*

The lecture was on Sieman's gas and glass furnaces. As the packed audience waited, Faraday shuffled onto the platform. His mind was not at its best. He accidentally scorched his notes on a burner prepared for a demonstration. Confused by this mishap, he forgot what he had planned to say. After several attempts to continue, he finally stammered, "I-I'm a-afraid I-I've been with you much too long. . . . The old c-candle is about to go out. . . ." Finding the last page of his notes, he managed, "I've lost my memory. My life has become a desert of dimness and forgetfulness. . . ."

Overcome with emotion, Faraday sank into his chair. His head was down. His eyes were swimming. A fraction of a second later, the entire audience was on its feet. Cheer after cheer shook the historic place, and many of those who cheered also wept. Deep inside they knew they were witnessing the sunset of England's greatest living scientist.

In 1864 Michael Faraday resigned his eldership in the Sandemanian church. Three years later, he gave up his position as superintendent of the laboratory in the R.I. From this time on, he spent much of his time in a chair facing the window in the house lent to him by Queen

Victoria. Sometimes his mind was clear. Often it was not.

It has been reported that on one occasion while Faraday's mind was lucid, some reporters questioned him concerning his "speculations" of life after death.

"Speculations!" he has been said to have exclaimed. "I know nothing about speculations. I'm resting on certainties. 'I know that my Redeemer liveth,' and because He lives I shall live also."

While sitting in his chair on August 25, 1867, he passed away. He was seventy-six.

He could have been buried in Westminster Abbey near his hero, Sir Isaac Newton, had he so desired. But he did not want this honor just as he did not want to be knighted. Instead, he was buried in a simple ceremony at Highgate Cemetery. The elders at his beloved church officiated at the simple ceremony. Thus, he was plain Michael Faraday right up to the end.

The notice on the inexpensive headstone reads:

MICHAEL FARADAY
Born 22 September 1791
Died 25 August 1867

EPILOGUE

Michael Faraday has been gone for well over a century. Considering his lack of formal education and the extremely crude instruments with which he worked, it is reasonable to ask if his breakthroughs have had any influence on our time.

The answer, of course, is an overwhelming yes. His surface work—those things that can be readily understood by the casual layman—are monumental. They include the dynamo, the transformer, the discovery of benzene, improvements in steel alloys, and a host of other things. But it must remembered that Faraday was more than an experimenter who worked with cut-and-try methods.

Michael Faraday was a philosopher and a first-class theoretician. Because of him modern scientists have the conception of the cutting of fields of force to generate electricity; the idea of space (Faraday's idea was most revolutionary, for his concept of empty space was in conflict with the theories of Newton); and his startling—for the time—belief in electrons and his suggestion as to how they work.

There were many behind-the-hand smiles when Faraday proclaimed the unity of force and matter and insisted these forces are interchangeable. Likewise, even learned men shook their heads in doubt when he proclaimed that light could be affected by magnetism. Today, thanks to Einstein, we know that Faraday was right.

Taking advantage of an eclipse of the sun on March 29, 1919, Einstein proved that light rays are bent by the forces of gravity. At that time, a bit of doggerel proclaimed:

> One thing is certain, and the rest debate—
> Light-rays when near the sun, do not go straight!

Had Faraday read that, he would have smiled. Why? Because he had proved that fact by demonstration nearly three quarters of a century before!

Faraday's Christian testimony has also helped mold people in modern times. The firmness of his faith and his determination to follow the Sermon on the Mount have influenced our age as much as or more than his studies on magnetism and electricity.

This testimony was demonstrated by him on many occasions.

While being interviewed at the Royal Institution, Faraday suddenly pointed to the portrait of Sir Humphry Davy. "There was a great man!" he exclaimed. Their sharp differences never marred Faraday's appreciation and respect for the man.

In our time, an electrical unit of capacity is known as a *farad*. That word honors Michael Faraday and his work in electricity. That his name is linked with a unit of capacity is a magnificent honor!

BIBLIOGRAPHY

Agassi, Joseph. *Faraday as a Natural Philosopher*. Chicago: University of Chicago Press, 1972.

Asimov, Isaac. *Breakthroughs in Science*. Boston: Houghton Mifflin, 1959.

Besant, Sir Walter. *London in the Eighteenth Century*. London, 1925.

_____. *London in the Time of the Stuarts*. London, 1903.

_____. *London in the Nineteenth Century*. London, 1910.

Carpenter, Edward. *A House of Kings: The Official History of Westminster Abbey*. New York: John Day, 1966.

Castelot, Andre. *Napoleon*. New York: Harper and Row, 1971.

Chancellor, E. Beresford. *Life in Regency and Early Victorian Times*. New York, Scribner's.

Cowie, L. W. *Plague and Fire: London 1665-66*. New York: Putnam, 1970.

Crowther, J. G. *Men of Science*. New York, 1936.

Dibner, Bern. *Oersted and the Discovery of Electromagnetism*. Blaisdell Publishing Co., 1962.

Faraday, Michael. *Experimental Researches in Chemistry and Physics*. London, 1859.

_____. *The Chemical History of a Candle*. New York: Harper and Brothers, 1899.

Hadfield, Sir Robert A. *Faraday and His Metallurgical Researches*. London: Chapman and Hall, 1931.

Hartley, Sir Harold. *Humphry Davy*. New York: Thomas Nelson, 1966.

James, Anthony Brett (compiler). *The Hundred Days*. New York: St. Martin's Press, 1964.

Jones, Bence. *The Life and Letters of Faraday* (2 Vols.) Longmans and Green, 1870.

Miller, Mabel. *Michael Faraday and the Dynamo*. Radnor, Pa.: Chilton Book Co., 1968.

Paris, John Ayrton, *Sir Humphry Davy*. London.

Patterson, Elizabeth; *John Dalton and the Atomic Theory*. New York: Doubleday, 1970.

Perkin Centennary: 100 Years of Dyestuffs. Elmsford, N.Y.: Pergamon Press, 1958.

Priestly, Joseph. *Autobiography of Joseph Priestly*. Cranbury, N.J.: Associated University Presses, 1970.

Record of the Royal Society of London. London: Morrison and Gibb, 1940.

Riedman, Sarah R. *Antoine Lavoisier, Scientist and Citizen*. New York: Thomas Nelson, 1957.

Sootin, Harry. *Michael Faraday: From Errand Boy to Master Physicist*. Julian Messner, 1954.

Spratt, Thomas. *Spratt's History of the Royal Society*. Washington University Studies, 1958.

Thomas, Henry, and Lee Thomas. *Living Biographies of Great Scientists*. Garden City Publishing Co., 1941.

Tilden, Sir William A. *Famous Chemists*. Facsimile edition. New York: Arno Press, 1921.

Tricker, R. A. *The Contributions of Faraday and Maxwell to Electrical Science*. Elmsford, N.Y.: Pergamon Press, 1966.

Tyndall, John. *Faraday as a Discoverer*. New York: Appleton, 1868.

Watts, Isaac. *Improvements of the Mind*. London.

Williams, Leslie P. *The Selected Correspondence of Michael Faraday* (2 Vols.), New York: Cambridge University Press.

Williams, L. Pearce. *Michael Faraday*. New York: Simon and Schuster, 1971.

Like Michael Faraday, **Author Charles Ludwig** had an extremely difficult time in pursuing his interest in the elementary principles of electricity. This was because his youth was spent with missionary parents in Kenya—two miles from the equator and hundreds of miles from the nearest electrical outlet.

But like his miracle-believing parents, he refused to give up. As a result, while others read by candles or smoky kerosine lanterns, he read the entire *World Book Encyclopedia* in a private room lit by flashlight bulbs twisted into empty can lids and powered by wornout flashlight batteries discarded by the missionaries. (Sometimes it took five or six of these discards connected together in a section of bamboo to equal the voltage of two fresh ones!)

Devouring all available books on electricity, he soon became interested in amateur radio. Again, persistence helped. This time he wound his own coils, manufactured his own batteries, and with a one-cylindered engine driving a discarded Chevrolet generator, developed enough power to operate his own radio station.

Using from ten to fifty watts of power and transmitting under the call letters VQ4KSL, he managed two-way communication with more than seventy countries.

Living with his wife, Mary, in Tucson, Arizona, Author Ludwig devotes most of his time to free-lance writing.